"YOU SEE," HE SAID AS HE ENDED THE KISS, "I CAN BE PASSIONATE."

"Passion is not the same thing as compassion."

"What an astute observation! But you're making a snap judgment about me. You don't know what I'm really like."

"I know you well enough. You care more about facts and figures than you do about people, Matt Royall," she declared angrily. "You practically said so yourself."

"No, you jumped to that conclusion simply because I tried to explain some painful realities to you. I'm being paid to choose the best site for an airport. The plateau behind your aunt's lodge may be it. So don't try to find someone to blame. This is an unfortunate situation where no one is at fault."

"I'll be sure to tell my aunt that. No doubt it will make her feel a lot better."

"Don't push me too far, Charlotte," he warned. "There's a limit to my patience, and you're coming close to overstepping the mark."

CANDLELIGHT ECSTASY ROMANCES®

QUANTITY SALES

Most Dell Books are available at special quantity discounts when purchased in bulk by corporations, organizations, and special-interest groups. Custom imprinting or excerpting can also be done to fit special needs. For details write: Dell Publishing Co., Inc., 1 Dag Hammarskjold Plaza, New York, NY 10017, Attn.: Special Sales Dept.,or phone: (212) 605-3319.

INDIVIDUAL SALES

Are there any Dell Books you want but cannot find in your local stores? If so, you can order them directly from us. You can get any Dell book in print. Simply include the book's title, author, and ISBN number, if you have it, along with a check or money order (no cash can be accepted) for the full retail price plus 75¢ per copy to cover shipping and handling. Mail to: Dell Readers Service, Dept. FM, P.O. Box 1000, Pine Brook, NJ 07058.

PLAYING WITH FIRE

Donna Kimel Vitek

A CANDLELIGHT ECSTASY ROMANCE®

Published by
Dell Publishing Co., Inc.
1 Dag Hammarskjold Plaza
New York, New York 10017

Dell ® TM 681510, Dell Publishing Co., Inc.

Candlelight Ecstasy Romance®, 1,203,540, is a registered
trademark of Dell Publishing Co., Inc., New York, New York.

ISBN: 0-440-16983-6

Printed in the United States of America

May 1986

10 9 8 7 6 5 4 3 2 1

WFH

To Our Readers:

We have been delighted with your enthusiastic response to Candlelight Ecstasy Romances®, and we thank you for the interest you have shown in this exciting series.

In the upcoming months we will continue to present the distinctive sensuous love stories you have come to expect only from Ecstasy. We look forward to bringing you many more books from your favorite authors and also the very finest work from new authors of contemporary romantic fiction.

As always, we are striving to present the unique, absorbing love stories that you enjoy most—books that are more than ordinary romance. Your suggestions and comments are always welcome. Please write to us at the address below.

Sincerely,

The Editors
Candlelight Romances
1 Dag Hammarskjold Plaza
New York, New York 10017

CHAPTER ONE

When the narrow winding road crested on a high hill, Charlotte Jordan slowed her blue Omni and gazed down at the scene below. Royal View was a small town nestled at the foot of the Rocky Mountains in Colorado. The silent rugged mountains, covered now with the green and golden aspens of early autumn, hadn't always been so peaceful. Once the majestic range that extended north into Wyoming had yielded fortunes in silver and made the town a center of feverish activity. Then the silver market had collapsed. In a mass exodus residents had gone away to seek wealth in distant gold fields, leaving Royal View to the few hardy citizens who remained to enjoy the mountains' rediscovered tranquility. Accelerating, Charlotte drove on, a slight frown marring her brow. River View looked different already. Since her childhood it had sprawled at the foot of the mountains, nostalgically untidy, three-fourths of its main street lined with deserted buildings. Now it looked as if those relics of the past were being methodically bulldozed and replaced with new buildings to give the town a neater appearance.

Progress, Charlotte thought with a resigned sigh as

the curving road led her down toward Royal View. Though she had to admit the town looked neater without most of the weathered gray buildings, she still would have preferred to see it the way it had always been—a bit decrepit perhaps, but a blessed oasis in a world that was becoming increasingly noisy and crowded. Besides, the town's new image served to re-enforce the claims Aunt Louisa had made in her last letter. She had stated in no uncertain terms that most of the county's residents had gone stark raving mad. They wanted to develop the pristine forests around them into a swanky resort area, she had written with bold strokes of her pen and many exclamation points, and they were actually contemplating using her own land to build a small airport to serve the wealthy tourists who would flock to the proposed resort hotels. And how would she stand it if the county did manage to force her to give up her beloved property? she had asked Charlotte.

Aunt Louisa's letter had seemed a call for help and Charlotte was answering it. She had left Colorado Springs early that morning, determined to do everything she could to see that her great aunt was not robbed of the land she had loved and lived on for fifty years. She and her late husband Will Jordan had built a rustic lodge in the hills above Royal View, and the secluded accommodations had been the favorite vacation spot for nature lovers for years. Though her great-aunt and uncle had barely eked out a living by running their lodge, they had been happy sharing the peace of the alpine forests, the clear blue mountain lakes, and the sun-washed vales that surrounded them. And if an airport was constructed on the plateau that overlooked the lodge, Charlotte knew all the peace and tranquility would be shattered. Aunt Louisa would be devastated by the loss. Getting on in years, and with a mild heart condition, she might never fully recover from the distress of watching her beloved surroundings swept away in a tide of progress.

As Charlotte drove slowly down the main street of Royal View a short time later, hope and determination glimmered in her emerald eyes. She certainly couldn't stop this county from becoming one huge resort, but she meant to try her best to see that her elderly great-aunt didn't suffer the consequences. She couldn't believe the county government had the right to force people to sell their property. But even if it did, surely the officials involved could be persuaded to locate the airport elsewhere.

With that hope in mind, Charlotte parked her car in front of the post office on Main Street. As she got out of the car and walked toward the door, she slipped on the jacket of her beige suit, glad to have its added warmth in the cooler mountain air. When she flicked her thick blond hair out from beneath the collar, it bounced around her shoulders, shimmering with silver highlights in the bright autumn sun. After smoothing her skirt, she entered the narrow office and approached the counter.

"Hello, Mrs. Taggart," Charlotte began, smiling hopefully. "I need some information. Could you give me the names of the county commissioners and tell me where I might find them?"

"Why, you're Louisa Jordan's niece, aren't you?" the gaunt fiftyish woman responded with a question of her own. "I would've known you anywhere, though

9

it's been ages since I saw you last. Why, you used to spend every summer up visiting Lou. Where have you been keeping yourself lately?"

Unperturbed by the friendly inquisition, Charlotte smiled. Tiny dimples appeared in her cheeks at each side of her softly curved mouth, and wry amusement danced in her wide green eyes. "Oh, I'm a free-lance artist in Colorado Springs now, so I only get to visit my aunt on occasional weekends. I don't make it to town very often. In fact, I'm surprised you recognized me."

"Well, why shouldn't I? You sure ain't changed much in the past few years. You look about the same now as you did when you were seventeen or eighteen," Mrs. Taggart declared flatly. "How old are you now? Twenty-one?"

"Twenty-three."

"Are you really? Don't time just fly by?" the post-mistress mused, clucking her tongue as she shook her head disbelievingly. "Seems like just yesterday when you'd come skipping barefoot in here with Lou, your hair all done up in pigtails and your face fairly covered with freckles." Pausing, she squinted as she carefully scrutinized Charlotte's smooth complexion. "And you still got a few scattered across your nose, don't you? Maybe that's why you still look about eighteen."

"Could be," Charlotte agreed hastily. "Now, about the commissioners—"

"Did you say you're an artist now?" Mrs. Taggart persisted curiously. "Are you one of them that paints those funny-looking pictures that don't look like much of anything? Leastwise, they don't to me."

Charlotte had to laugh as she shook her head. "My

10

paintings are very simple. I design greeting cards for a young couple who've just started their own small business. They like the kind of nature scenes I paint."

Mrs. Taggart's brown eyes widened. "Say now, I got the prettiest Christmas card from Lou last year. It was a lone pine tree in the snow. Was it one you did?" When Charlotte nodded, the postmistress expressed her approval with a jerky bobbing of her head. "Well, it was real nice. Reminded me so much of places I've seen round here all my life."

"Thank you," Charlotte replied. "I can't imagine painting anything other than natural scenes. I guess Aunt Louisa's love of the land was bound to rub off on me. Speaking of the land, I do need to see the county commissioners, if you could tell me where to find them."

"To tell the truth, I don't even know their names," the postmistress confessed without apology. "They don't live here in town, so I don't have no reason to keep up with them. But I reckon Lou does. I know she's all stirred up about the airport they're wanting to build. Is that why you want to talk to them?"

"I hope they'll be able to tell me that they're only considering the plateau above the lodge as a possible site. There must be other places in the county where they could locate this new airport."

"I wouldn't know about that, but maybe the mayor would," Mrs. Taggart suggested. "You know him—Gilbert Kelly. Owns the gas station."

Nodding, Charlotte thanked the postmistress for the information and hurried out to the street. Deciding it would be quicker to walk to the gas station than moving her car, she passed by the combination grocery-

11

hardware store, then the tiny café that still sported starched white curtains on the window, as it had when she was a child. The facades of both establishments gleamed with coats of recently applied paint, as if their owners were anticipating the tourist boom that would come if the county did indeed become a resort mecca. Catching her lower lip between her teeth, Charlotte realized that most of the residents of Royal View would welcome a sharp increase in business. Actually, she had no quarrel with them about that. She simply didn't want their plans to allow her aunt to lose everything she loved, especially when the proposed airport could undoubtedly be located in a place where no one would be hurt and everyone who wanted development could still reap the benefits.

Stepping onto the cracked and pitted concrete apron that surrounded the gas station, Charlotte ran a smoothing hand over her hair. Pausing a moment, she looked around for some sign of life, but the station looked as deserted as the rest of the town did. Seeing no one in the darkened service bay, she started toward the office, the low heels of her navy pumps tapping lightly on the cement. The distinct yet not unpleasant smell of gasoline and motor oil lingered in the air around the pumps, and she smiled as she stopped in front of the office. The door was standing ajar, giving her a clear view of the honorable mayor snoozing peacefully in a rickety swivel chair, his feet propped up on a terribly cluttered desk. When she coughed softly to gain his attention, he awakened with a start and allowed his feet to fall to the floor as he sat up.

If he recognized her, he didn't mention it, so Charlotte immediately introduced herself. When he quickly averted his gaze and began to fidget, then raked his fingers through his sparse salt and pepper hair, Charlotte added warily, "Mrs. Taggart thought you might be able to give me the names of the county commissioners. I need to get in touch with them."

His expression was solemn. "Well, I'll give you their names, Charlotte, but I don't think it'll do you much good to see them if you're going to talk about the new county airport," he announced somewhat apologetically. Stuffing his hands into the pockets of his well-worn work pants, he faced her directly again. "You have to understand something, honey. Most everybody in this county is for building that airport. I just wish your aunt could see it the way the rest of us do. We're in bad need of money around here and resort development would bring in tax revenues. It would also give the young folks work when they graduate from school. Now, nearly all of them have to leave home to find jobs. Whole families have moved away. You can't much blame them. People have to work to eat and there's few places to work around here."

"I understand all that. Really, I do," Charlotte assured him, concern darkening her eyes. "And I think Aunt Louisa understands it too, but you have to understand that she's very scared right now. She's afraid the new airport's going to be located on the plateau above her lodge, and that's why I want to see the commissioners. It would be such a relief to be able to tell her that they're considering other sites too. They are considering others, aren't they?"

"One or two," Mayor Kelly muttered as he shifted his feet. Then he spread his hand in a resigned gesture. "But I have to tell you the truth. That plateau above

13

your aunt's place is beginning to look like the best site. And when it comes down to a final decision, the commissioners are likely to follow the advice of the civil engineer who's heading up this project. I just don't think it would do you much good to talk to any of them."

"Well, I intend to speak to someone," Charlotte declared with a defiant lift of her chin. "Since no final decision's been made, maybe it would help if I saw the engineer who's in charge of everything. If I could make him understand how Aunt Louisa feels about—"

"Engineers can't afford to be understanding sometimes, honey," the mayor warned her, his lips twisting with regret. "They have to look at all the facts and make a decision based on numbers, not on folks' feelings. It's a shame, but that's the way it is."

"Even so, I want to talk to the engineer," Charlotte persisted, unwilling to be swayed from her objective. "Surely he can't be as cold and unfeeling as you're trying to make him sound. If there's another site for the airport, he'll just have to take Aunt Louisa's feelings into consideration and choose it. Where can I find him now? I want to talk to him right away, before I see my aunt."

"Well, if that's really what you want to do, I guess you can give it a try," Mayor Kelly said, though his tone conveyed unmistakable doubts. "Matthew Royall's the engineer's name, and I believe he and his crew are up surveying the plateau this afternoon. It hasn't rained here lately, so you ought to be able to get up that old road in a car."

"Thanks for telling me where to find him," Charlotte said, smiling as she politely extended her right hand, which was immediately enclosed in the mayor's much larger one. When he didn't release her at once and appeared to want to say something more, her soft brown eyebrows lifted questioningly.

"Just don't set your heart on influencing Matthew Royall," he finally advised. "It may be that he'll have to choose that plateau behind your aunt's place for the airport because it's the best site. Now, nobody in this town respects Louisa Jordan more than I do, and I'm hoping that airport will be built on one of the other sites just for her sake. But if that can't be, maybe you can manage to convince her that sometimes things just have to be done for the good of the community."

"I'm sure Aunt Louisa does understand that," Charlotte assured him softly, despite the adamant glimmer of rebellion that flared briefly in her eyes. Squaring her shoulders, she extracted her hand from his. "But I certainly don't want to see my aunt become the sacrificial lamb in this situation, and I plan to do everything in my power to prevent that from happening. I hope you and the rest of the county can understand that."

As the mayor nodded rather unhappily, Charlotte said good-bye and walked briskly to her car. Once inside she inserted the key in the ignition, then paused a moment, her hands tightly gripping the steering wheel. Mayor Kelly hadn't exactly been encouraging in his comments, yet she knew she couldn't let his pessimism deter her from doing what she had come to do. Her aunt needed her, she reminded herself, as she slowly backed out into the deserted street.

The paved highway forked just beyond some recently leveled buildings at the end of town, and Charlotte took the graveled road to the right, relaxing somewhat as the route led up into the hills. Woods soon enclosed her on both sides, and the spreading branches of the trees that bordered the road entangled in a canopy overhead. The turning leaves of the aspens glimmered like blankets of undulating gold in a gentle breeze. Between their slender, smooth gray trunks, Charlotte caught occasional glimpses of a stream. It seemed a shame to feel discontent amidst such serene beauty, and when she drove past the curving drive that led to her aunt's lodge, she wished with all her heart that this unfortunate situation had never arisen. Charlotte wasn't a fighter by nature, and she had no desire to take on the entire county. Yet some things were worth fighting for, and this was one of them. Her aunt's happiness and health were being threatened, and if Charlotte herself didn't speak up for her, it looked as if no one else would.

The condition of the graveled road deteriorated as she drove. It finally became no more than a rutted track leading to the plateau. Shifting down to first gear, Charlotte bounced along, thinking this was a perfectly ridiculous place to even consider locating an airport. Yet Mayor Kelly had been right in guessing that the engineer and his crew were here today, because the vegetation that had encroached on the bumpy road was flattened as if someone had recently driven over it. When she rounded the last curve and bumped over the final steep rise to reach the flat land, she had to brake quickly to avoid running into the back of one of the trucks parked directly in her way.

More than a little relieved that the uncomfortable

drive had ended, Charlotte hurriedly switched off the engine, then got out, grimacing when her left shoe slipped on a small patch of mud. Pumps were certainly not the footgear for hiking over terrain like this, but she had dressed up to make a good impression on the county commissioners when she talked to them. If she had known she would be forced to come trekking up here in search of an engineer and his surveying crew, she would have worn jeans and her hiking boots. But she hadn't known, and there was nothing she could do about it now.

Circling around the trucks and the two Jeeps parked ahead of them, Charlotte stopped short as she saw the group of people standing in the center of the long, wide plateau. Beyond them the surveying team was setting up a transit by the narrow border of trees toward the end of the plateau, where it began to slope up into the adjoining hill. Charlotte's heart sank. They certainly were acting as if they were seriously considering this site. It was easily long and wide enough to provide room for a small airfield, hangars, and a terminal building.

"Why couldn't it be smaller?" she muttered bleakly. When she had been a child, the vastness of the plateau had delighted her. She had spent countless hours up here, running through the grass, chasing butterflies and picking bouquets of delicate blue columbines. All those lovely memories washed over her now and a suspicious tightness constricted her throat. She could hardly bear to think of such an exquisite playground being covered with concrete, consigned to just a memory. Her hands balled into tight fists at her sides as resentment filled her, resentment toward these intruding strangers who suddenly had the power to decide whether this plateau was ruined or was left as nature had designed it. Yet it was a resentment she fought to suppress, knowing she must be diplomatic in dealing with this Matthew Royall.

After taking several deep, calming breaths, she started toward the group. The browning grass rustled beneath her feet, but no one seemed to notice her approach until a partially exposed root nearly tripped her and she gasped.

Charlotte bit back an irritated oath when she glanced up and found all eyes turned in her direction. Feeling more than a little inept, she bent down to withdraw the dried stalk of a weed that had pierced one leg of her pantyhose near her knee. As she walked on, she winced with every step she took as a large run feathered up her thigh and down her calf. She trudged on anyway, a weak little smile tugging at her lips.

A tall, beautiful brunette, the lone woman of the group, stepped forward without smiling to block Charlotte's path. "If you're lost, I suggest you just drive back to the main highway and try to get your bearings. You can't be interested in anything on this road, obviously, since this is the end of it."

"I'm not lost, actually," Charlotte informed her, excusing herself as she swiftly sidestepped the woman and inclined her head in greeting to the three men in the group. Turning toward the eldest, who was dressed in a suit and had graying hair, she smiled hesitantly. "Mayor Kelly suggested I speak with you, Mr. Royall. I'm—" Her words broke off as a large bronzed hand abruptly descended on her left forearm and she was slowly turned toward one of the younger men. Tall

18

and muscularly lean, he was thirty-five or so, with sun-streaked sandy blond hair. Clear and coolly intelligent dark amber eyes looked her over, registering a faint glimmer of amusement when they lingered on her torn hose, and she involuntarily tried to hide that offending leg behind the other.

"I'm Matt Royall," he said at last, his deep voice pleasantly modulated, his tone polite. The strongly carved features of his tanned face conveyed no readable expression as he stepped toward her, looking down into her emerald eyes as they widened with surprise.

Charlotte could only stare up at him, unprepared for a Matthew Royall who looked like this. Clad in jeans and a denim jacket, he looked more like one of the surveying crew than the chief engineer who held Aunt Louisa's future in his hands. Now that she was face to face with him, she didn't know how to begin saying what she had to say.

"I repeat—I'm Matt Royall," he prompted as her silence continued. "And you're . . ."

"Oh. Charlotte Jordan," she hastened to introduce herself. "I'm Louisa Jordan's niece. I want to talk to you about this airport you're planning. This site—"

"This site looks to be the best one in the county, young lady," the older man interjected huffily. "And nothing your aunt's told you to come up here and say is going to change that fact. I'm Joe Fletcher, one of the county commissioners, and that woman's been after me for weeks to stop the surveying up here, but I can't do it. Louisa Jordan's just going to have to understand that we've got to start developing the land around here. Just think what they did in Vail. They

19

turned a sheep meadow into one of the finest resorts in the country. If they could do it, we can too. But we need an airport, and if it has to be located on this plateau, then that's just the way it has to be."

Charlotte's face reflected her inner dismay. There was a discernible hint of appeal in her eyes as they sought Matt Royall's expressionless face. "You mean you've made a decision already?" she whispered urgently. "You really plan to locate the airport up here?"

"No decision's been made," he stated emphatically, his strong jaw tightening with some impatience as he glanced at the commissioner. Yet there was nothing about his demeanor that Charlotte found particularly reassuring as he turned his steady gaze on her again. In fact, there was a distinct coolness in his eyes as he widened his stance and flicked back the sides of his jacket to place his hands on narrow hips. "The truth of the matter is that I probably won't be making a decision for several weeks. I think it would be better if we discussed this later, Ms. Jordan."

"Oh, but I need to talk to you now. Aunt Louisa's so upset about this," Charlotte attempted to explain. "And she's such a fine woman. If you only knew her—"

"I do know your aunt. She's a fine woman, and I know she's upset about the possibility that the airfield might be located up here," Matt interrupted, a certain hard edge in his voice as he shook his head. "But as I said, now's not the time to discuss the matter. I'm very busy."

"I'm sure you are, and I really hate to bother you, but—"

"Later, Ms. Jordan. I want my surveyors to finish

the grade of the western boundary, so I don't have time for you now. When I do have time, I'll let you know and we can discuss your aunt's problem then."

Charlotte doubted that, and her doubts must have shown. When she opened her mouth to tell him she didn't appreciate the way he dismissed her so quickly, a warning light flared in his tawny eyes and she snapped her mouth shut, unwilling to antagonize him further. Unluckily, he held all the cards in this situation. He had the power to hurt her aunt if Charlotte was foolish enough to lash out at him for his superior attitude.

Counting mentally to ten, she controlled her temper, but it took all the self-control she could muster to say with any semblance of politeness, "Very well. You can contact me at my aunt's lodge when you have time. But if you haven't contacted me in a few days, I may have to come looking for you again. Do you understand?"

He understood perfectly, it seemed. As if she had come right out and said she didn't trust him, he stared at her, his eyes narrowing. Then a rather mocking smile tugged at the corners of his firm mouth. "I'll be in touch, Ms. Jordan," he said, his voice low, his words clipped and precise.

Charlotte stared right back at him, unable to prevent the sudden defiant thrust of her small chin. And when that involuntary gesture elicited a knowing grin from him, warmth suffused her cheeks, then spread over every inch of her skin, which made her more susceptible to the brisk wind that suddenly kicked up, swirling flaxen wisps of hair against her hot cheeks.

21

The cool air permeated the loose weave of her suit, and she shivered.

"I'm sure your aunt wouldn't want you to risk catching a cold, Ms. Jordan," Matt Royall said expressionlessly. "So, as I said, we'll discuss this later."

As he turned away and began speaking to the surveyor, Charlotte's hopes fell a bit. And her confidence wasn't helped in the least by the cool emotionless smile on the statuesque brunette, who embodied casual elegance in her tailored camel slacks, lavender cashmere sweater, and tweed jacket. Pretending to ignore her superior smirk, Charlotte strolled away from the group. By the time she reached her car, she realized the task she had taken on promised to be a great deal more difficult than she had imagined. Matt Royall hadn't acted particularly interested in hearing anything she had to say.

CHAPTER TWO

Once in her car Charlotte felt warm again—too warm.
The mere remembrance of Matt Royall's sardonic attitude was enough to induce the reappearance of a rosy
blush in her cheeks. He had nerve trying to con her
into believing he would be in touch with her soon,
when she knew very well that he wouldn't. But if he
thought he would be rid of her once and for all with
his obvious brush-off, he had better think again. Charlotte was no quitter, and she intended to talk to him
about her aunt if she had to chase him all over the
county to do it.

Righteous determination compressed her lips as she
started her car and turned it around to begin the peril-
ous descent from the plateau. Riding the brake as she
negotiated the curves in the rutted road, she gripped
the steering wheel so tightly that her knuckles were
white. Thus far in her mission to protect her aunt's
interests, she had met with no success. Though Mayor
Kelly had expressed his great respect for Louisa Jordan, he had shown no inclination to come to her de-
fense in her battle to preserve her land. The county
commissioner had been so obviously unsympathetic to
Louisa's position, that Charlotte knew without a

doubt they could expect no help from him. As for Matt Royall, he had exhibited something akin to cold indifference, and his refusal to even discuss the matter with Charlotte was discouraging and upsetting. She could only say a little prayer that he wouldn't truly prove to be an emotionless businessman who never considered people, but based his decisions solely on facts. Somehow Charlotte had to make him understand her great-aunt's love for the land.

Refusing to give in to the rising pessimism she was feeling, Charlotte forced herself to relax. After switching on the radio to a station that played soothing music, she leaned back in her seat, determined to focus her immediate attention on the beauty surrounding her. The ruts in the road became a series of bumps that eventually smoothed out enough so she no longer had to clutch the steering wheel with both hands to keep the car on course. When she turned onto the narrow winding drive that led to her aunt's lodge, she felt a sense of contentment steal over her, easing even more of her tension. She loved this land almost as much as her aunt did, and would always be grateful to her parents for allowing her to spend most of her childhood summers here. Though they had visited Aunt Louisa as often as they possibly could, Charlotte's father's business had kept him and her mother in Pueblo most of the time, except for an occasional weekend. Yet they had wanted Charlotte to learn to appreciate the joys of nature, so they brought her up to stay with Louisa and Will Jordan, though they had missed not having her at home. Charlotte had missed them too, yet oddly enough, she had never felt homesick during the summers she spent here. Instead she had always felt she was where she belonged. Even now, though she was older and could no longer spend her summers here, she still felt a sense of oneness with the mountains.

Charlotte smiled as a light breeze rustled through the trees bordering the long drive, and when a shower of golden aspen leaves drifted down onto the hood of her car, she opened her window slightly and appreciatively inhaled the fragrant autumn air. Her heartbeat quickened a bit in anticipation as the winding lane ascended a thickly wooded hill, and when she reached the crest, she was able to see her first glimpse of the lodge in which she had spent so many happy hours. Her great-aunt and uncle had built their home themselves. A sprawling two-story structure, constructed of rough-hewn logs, it almost seemed a part of the surrounding woodlands. Behind it rose the steep craggy mountain that leveled at its peak to form the plateau, but from such a distance away, Charlotte could see no sign of Matt Royall's surveying crew, much to her relief. She had no desire to think about those intruders now, when she would soon be seeing her great-aunt for the first time in several weeks.

Deciding she wouldn't even mention her encounter with Matthew Royall, Charlotte pulled up in front of the lodge and parked in the pebbled area provided for guest's vehicles. A silver BMW was already parked there, eliciting surprise in Charlotte. She wasn't accustomed to seeing such luxurious automobiles in an out-of-the-way place like this. Her aunt's guests usually drove station wagons or campers that were equipped to be driven over rough terrain, but she supposed the owners of the BMW could be at the lodge to take advantage of the hiking trails nearby. Or perhaps they had merely come to soak up the peaceful atmosphere.

After switching off the engine and removing her key from the ignition, Charlotte got out of her car and stood for a moment, enthralled by the muted sounds of the forest. The dying leaves of the trees rustled in the gentle wind, and the spreading dark green boughs of the evergreens whispered hauntingly as they brushed against one another. From overhead came the distant call of birds flying south for the winter. Mesmerized, Charlotte was scarcely aware that the air was becoming increasingly cooler now that the sun was sinking toward the western horizon. But when a playful breeze feathered through her hair to chill the nape of her neck, she shivered, roused herself from her pleasant reverie, and proceeded to remove her luggage from the back of her car.

Since she hadn't known exactly how long this visit would last, she had brought along more of her belongings than she usually did. Yet she managed to carry the two suitcases and tote bag to the veranda in only one trip, and even succeeded in opening the door, before her largest suitcase slipped from her grasp and landed with a loud bang on the hardwood floor.

The crashing sound Charlotte's suitcase made brought her immediate attention. Across the spacious public room the swinging door beside the huge stone fireplace suddenly flew open and Louisa Jordan bounded out of the kitchen, moving with a spry gait that belied her seventy-four years. Despite her avid love of nature, she was not the robust outdoor type of woman most people expected her to be. Louisa Jordan was tiny, even shorter than Charlotte, who could only be described as petite.

Yet as small as she herself was, Charlotte experienced a keen sense of protectiveness as she hurried across the room to meet the older woman. Aunt Louisa's hair seemed whiter than it had when Charlotte last saw her, and the lines in her face appeared to be more deeply etched. And as Charlotte was enfolded in seemingly frail arms and kissed enthusiastically on one cheek, she felt an inner resentment that this fine elderly lady was about to do battle with an entire county. Charlotte longed to pat her aunt's back and assure her she had arrived to solve all her problems for her, yet she knew Louisa Jordan better than to say that. Despite her age and seeming frailty, Aunt Louisa was a strong independent woman, capable of waging her own battles. In her fight with the county, she would need Charlotte only as an ally, not a protectress. Realizing that fact, Charlotte bit back words of sympathy and simply returned her great-aunt's kiss.

"You look marvelous as usual, Aunt Lou," she said after finally being released from a surprisingly strong hug. Then she grinned and touched her fingertips to the older woman's lined cheeks. "But I can guess what you were doing when I came in—making your famous sourdough biscuits for dinner. You have flour streaked over your face."

"A little flour never hurt anybody," Louisa replied, wiping away the flour with the corner of her apron. Taking one step back, she subjected her grand-niece to a thorough examination, then shook her head as a frown further marked her lined brow. "But what's happened to you, honey? You got a run in your stock-

27

ing that's about as wide as a railroad track. What did you do—stop on the way here to have a fight with a grizzly bear?"

"Nothing so dramatic," Charlotte answered laughingly. "Would you believe a dried flower stalk actually did all this damage? Of course, they're brand new and everybody knows you only have to look at a new pair the wrong way to get a run in them."

Louisa nodded. "Used to have the same problem with silk stockings. Seemed like the more they cost, the more apt they were to get runs in them. But never mind that. Why are you so dressed up anyway? And aren't you a little late getting here? When I talked to you last night, you said you'd be here by midafternoon."

"Well, I got a late start, and the traffic was heavier than I thought it would be," Charlotte answered evasively, unwilling to tell her aunt about her futile discussions with the mayor and Matt Royall. Seeking to change the subject completely, she gestured back toward the front door of the lodge. "I saw the BMW parked out there. I guess the lodge's reputation is finally reaching the wealthy set. Are you making your sourdough biscuits in honor of prestigious guests?"

"Rich or poor, all my guests get those biscuits, because I like them myself. And in all the years we've had folks coming here, nobody's complained yet. Not even anybody who drives a fancy car like an MGW."

"BMW," Charlotte corrected, smiling fondly at her aunt's indifference to the trappings of wealth. Louisa found joy in simple pleasures and nature, which was why an airport built practically on top of her would shatter her peaceful life. With an inward sigh, Char-

28

lotte temporarily pushed that considerable problem to the back of her mind and glanced at the bare hardwood stairs that led up to the second floor. "Well, since you're busy preparing dinner, I'll just go up and change my clothes, then be right down to give you a hand."

Louisa nodded, then briefly hugged her niece again. "Thank you for coming up, honey," she said softly. "I know you did it because I was so upset when I last wrote you, and I feel a little guilty about dragging you away from that nice young man of yours."

"No need to feel guilty, Aunt Lou. Brad and I aren't seeing each other now, anyway," Charlotte said with a grim smile that didn't reach her eyes. "Brad's boss at the ad agency introduced him to his daughter, and Brad decided she has more to offer than I do."

"Oh dear," Louisa murmured, surveying Charlotte's face carefully, as if she expected to find her innermost feelings exhibited there. "I would never have suspected Brad of being an opportunist. He seemed so fond of you."

"Apparently not fond enough," Charlotte replied ruefully. "He certainly didn't mind dropping me when the boss's daughter came along."

"Well then, that's his loss," Louisa pronounced tartly, giving Charlotte's arm a reassuring squeeze. "Just you remember that all men aren't like Brad, so don't be too hurt by all this."

"I think it's mostly my pride that's wounded," Charlotte admitted. "Though I did think my relationship with Brad might have developed into something serious, I hadn't gotten too deeply involved with him,

29

so I'm not feeling terribly hurt. I'm more irritated especially at myself for not seeing how shallow he was."

"Well," Louisa counseled gently, "the man for you will come along soon, I'm sure of it."

"Well, until he does, I plan to steer clear of the ambitious type who puts his career above everything else," Charlotte said emphatically, then dismissed the entire subject with a toss of one hand. "Now, enough of that. You get back to your biscuits and I'll go change so I can help you with dinner."

After Louisa nodded agreeably and went back into the kitchen, Charlotte gathered up her luggage and proceeded up the varnished stairs. She followed the flower-printed runner down the wide hallway to the southern end of the house. A door stood ajar, inviting her into the room she had always occupied on her visits. She smiled to herself as she entered, feeling at home within the knotted pine walls. It was a room more comfortable than elegant, though there was grace in the simple design of the four-poster bed and the dresser that matched it. Gaily colored hooked rugs were scattered on the polished hardwood floor, and lacy crocheted curtains covered two tall narrow windows. Outside, a thicket of aspens sloped upward in a diagonal toward the plateau, their golden leaves forming a gem of topaz in the setting of surrounding evergreens. A rock-strewn stream beyond the trees tumbled toward a distant creek, which in turn would help feed the Colorado River, and Charlotte wondered what would happen to all the little brooks if indiscriminate development began to mar the county.

Pensively nibbling her lower lip, she turned from the window. Deciding to leave unpacking until later, she laid her large suitcase on the chest at the foot of the high bed and opened it to extract a pair of jeans and a cable-knit sweater. She changed clothes quickly, and after hanging her suit in the closet, left the room.

In the spacious country kitchen, Louisa was bent down beside the open oven, taking out a pan of golden-brown biscuits. Her cheeks were rosy from the heat and still smudged with flour, but there was a contented light in her eyes as she transferred the biscuits from pan to cloth-lined basket. Happy as she always was when she prepared a meal, she was humming softly to herself when she looked up and saw Charlotte standing beside the wooden chopping block in the center of the kitchen, her thumbs hooked into the back pockets of her jeans. She smiled warmly.

"I'll make the salad," said Charlotte, returning the smile as she went to the refrigerator for the vegetables. She mixed both Romaine and iceberg lettuce in a large wooden bowl, then added chunks of the last of summer's tomatoes and thinly sliced mushrooms. While tossing lightly, she took a deep breath and exhaled it as a dreamy sigh. "I always feel so alive when I'm up here," she commented. "I guess it must be the mountain air that's so invigorating."

"I think it's the quiet. The fresh air's nice, all right, but it wouldn't mean much if it wasn't so peaceful here. You can get to know yourself in a place like this, and feel like you belong. I don't think I could ever stand to live anyplace else. Towns give me the jitters, everything's so noisy and . . ." Louisa's words halted and anguish settled for an instant in her face, then she shook her head and laughed humorlessly. "Well, I ex-

31

pect I'll have to get used to lots of noise if they build the airport up on the plateau."

"Are you absolutely alone in this, Aunt Lou?" Charlotte asked somberly. "Surely there are other people around here who don't want to see an airport built on that plateau? It is something of a local landmark."

"I'm sorry to say old landmarks don't seem to mean much if they stand in the way of progress," Louisa said sadly. "Even some of my oldest friends, though they know how I feel and sympathize, would like to see the county developed. They feel that if the plateau turns out to be the best site for the airport, that's where it has to be built."

"Maybe they'll find a better site," Charlotte offered hopefully. "That could happen."

Smiling gratefully at her niece, Louisa shook her head. "It's sweet of you to try to cheer me, but I know how interested the county commissioners are in the plateau. I'm not going to give up yet on trying to convince them another site would be better, but I know I'm fighting an uphill battle."

"You can't lose hope, Aunt Lou."

"And I can't build false hopes either," Lou replied, opening a jar of homegrown peas and pearl onions she had preserved. As she started to pour them into a saucepan, she suddenly went still and turned her head to one side to listen. Moments later the front door of the lodge was opened and footsteps sounded on the floor. Louisa nodded. "Thought I heard the Jeep. Our guests are back, so we'll have dinner in half an hour. Let's get busy."

Twenty minutes later, while Louisa was checking the succulent trout fillets broiling in the oven, she glanced toward the kitchen door, then turned to Charlotte. "I hear somebody out there. Play hostess for me, honey, since you're not covered with flour like I am. Go out and see if they'd like something to drink before dinner."

After one last look at the simmering peas, Charlotte slipped off her apron and hurried from the kitchen into the public room, then halted in midstride with a startled gasp as she nearly collided with a man standing near the fireplace. Strong hands lightly clasped her upper arms to steady her.

"I'm sorry. I didn't expect anyone to be standing here," she murmured, her gaze traveling up from a black sweater on a broad chest to a chiseled sunbrowned face she immediately recognized. Except for the flicker of surprise that appeared in her green eyes, she showed no visible reaction at finding herself practically in Matt Royall's arms. She automatically took a backward step, relieved when he released his hold on her.

"Well, Mr. Royall, I must say I'm surprised you came to see me," she announced flatly. "You didn't seem all that interested in what I had to say about the airport this afternoon. Frankly, I thought I'd have to chase you all over the county in order to talk to you about my aunt."

A cool smile touched his mouth. "Sorry to disappoint you, Ms. Jordan, but I'm not here to see you. I'm a guest at the lodge."

"A guest? *Here?*" she exclaimed softly, too disconcerted by this bit of news to maintain composure completely. Slipping her fingers through the thick blond hair that grazed her temple, she shook her head as if

33

to reassemble her thoughts. She folded her arms across her chest and managed to say without overt hostility, "This is an interesting state of affairs, isn't it? Tell me, does my aunt know who you are and why you're here?"

"She knew who I was and why I'd come before I even introduced myself," Matt answered, a more genuine smile curving his lips. "Your aunt's a very perceptive lady. She may be isolated in this lodge, but she still manages to know everything that's going on in the county. Even if I'd bothered to try hiding my identity, I wouldn't have succeeded. Surely you realize that? Louisa Jordan's no fool."

"No, she isn't, but neither am I, Mr. Royall," Charlotte said crisply. "And I don't really appreciate the fact that you didn't bother to tell me you were staying at the lodge when I spoke to you this afternoon. I might have been more inclined to believe you when you said we'd discuss the proposed airport at a later time."

"An oversight on my part. I'm sorry," he apologized, slipping his long-fingered hands into the pockets of his gray corduroys while surveying her carefully. "It simply never occurred to me to mention I was staying here. But you did catch me at a very busy moment."

"You're not busy now," Charlotte said, lowering her voice so her aunt couldn't overhear. "So let's talk about the airport. If you only knew how important your decision is going to be to Aunt Lou—"

"This isn't the right time to begin this discussion either," he interrupted softly yet firmly. His expression was neither encouraging nor discouraging; it was simply unreadable. But there was no mistaking his implacable tone as he continued, "Since it's nearly time for dinner, I see no point in beginning a conversation we can't finish."

"I only want to tell you how disturbed Aunt Lou is. It won't take me a great deal of time to say what I have to say."

"I imagine it'll take more time than you think," he replied. "Because of your aunt, you're emotionally involved in this situation, and when emotions are involved, discussions tend to get lengthy."

"Maybe you're right," Charlotte murmured reluctantly, unable in all honesty to argue with his logic. She nodded. "Okay, we'll talk later. After dinner might be the perfect time. Now, Aunt Lou sent me out to offer you a drink. May I get you something?"

"Scotch and water would be fine."

"And I'd just love some white wine," a lilting voice called out from the stairway.

Without surprise, Charlotte turned to watch the tall brunette who had been with Matt on the plateau float down the steps, a vision of elegance in a white silk blouse and a floor-length black skirt. She glided across the room with a casual toss of her head that sent her thick raven hair swirling against her cheeks. Giving Matt a sultry smile, she clasped her hands around his upper right arm and announced in a stage whisper, "I just felt like dressing for dinner tonight. A woman should look her best in the evenings, don't you think?"

Though Charlotte couldn't fail to notice the disparaging glance cast at her own jeans and sweater, she smiled politely, playing the perfect hostess.

"Ms. Jordan, this is Didi Talbot," Matt introduced

the brunette. "And of course, we saw Mrs. Jordan's niece, Charlotte, on the plateau this afternoon."

Moving closer to Matt, Didi gave Charlotte a dazzling pretense of a smile that did nothing to defrost her appraising stare. She inclined her head but said nothing, apparently feeling the gesture itself sufficed.

"It's nice to meet you, Ms. Talbot," Charlotte said softly, then turned toward the bar. As she poured a measure of Scotch into a tumbler, then added water and ice, she supposed she was expected to feel intimidated by Didi. It was obvious that Didi wanted her to feel that way, but Charlotte had dealt with pretentious women before, so this one didn't upset her equilibrium. She handed the couple their drinks, advised them that dinner would be served within minutes, and walked unhurriedly into the kitchen.

"Was that Matt who came down?" Louisa asked, busily moving from oven to counter to worktable, putting finishing touches on the meal. "I hope the two of you introduced yourselves."

"I met Mr. Royall this afternoon, Aunt Lou," Charlotte confessed, and went on to explain her visit to the mayor and the futile trek up to the plateau. When she finished, she shrugged. "I didn't mention this to you earlier because I didn't really get to talk to him. He was very busy."

"They were surveying up there today; I knew they planned to," Louisa said, worry passing like a shadow over her face. "Matt's a very hard-working young man, but I hope you'll get a chance to talk to him. He's really pleasant."

Surprise lifted Charlotte's delicate eyebrows as she placed salad plates on a tray. "You sound as if you like

36

Mr. Royall, Aunt Lou. To tell the truth, I was amazed to learn you're even allowing him to stay at the lodge. I didn't think you'd want him here. After all, he is the man who may make the decision to build the airport on the plateau."

"He hasn't decided yet, so I'm not giving up hope," Louisa said adamantly, then lowered her voice to a whisper. "Besides, I think it's wise to let him stay here. That way, I always know what he's up to."

Charlotte had to laugh. "Aunt Lou, I never realized you were so shrewd, not to mention sneaky. How do you manage to know what he's up to?"

"I ask him. You know I've always liked to keep track of my guests' whereabouts. Some of them have gotten lost on hikes, but since I've known where they planned to be, I could tell the searchers where to start looking. It's quite natural for me to ask Matt every morning where he plans to go."

"Somehow I can't imagine Matt Royall and his entire surveying crew getting lost."

"Better safe than sorry, I always say," Louisa murmured. "Anyway, I'm sure he knows I have another reason to want to know where he is."

"You've told him that an airport so close to the lodge would ruin the secluded atmosphere? How did he react?"

"He always listens carefully when I talk to him. He even seems to understand how I feel. I think he's sympathetic but . . ." Louisa sighed somewhat despondently. "He never really says anything to reassure me."

One of those emotionless men who never let people get in the way of his career, Charlotte thought, wrinkling her nose disdainfully. She had suspected Matt Royall was like that, and hearing her suspicions confirmed by her aunt only strengthened her resolve to try and make him truly understand how Louisa felt. Charlotte knew she could say what Louisa might be too proud to tell him, that since the death of her husband running the lodge had become the purpose in her life. No one had the right to take that away, and Charlotte intended to tell him so. She hoped he would prove reasonable, but if he didn't, she was prepared to fight for her aunt.

Slipping her arm around Louisa's shoulders, she gave her a quick hug and a kiss on the cheek. "Don't worry, okay? As you said, Mr. Royall hasn't made a decision yet, so we have lots of time to try to influence his thinking. Besides, there may be another site in the county more suitable for an airfield."

"Nobody else seems to think there is." Louisa wearily massaged her left shoulder and shook her head. "From what I hear, all the county commissioners are real excited because the plateau is so centrally located."

"But there are so many other factors to consider," Charlotte reminded her. Deciding it was time to change the subject, she asked, "Who's this Didi who tags after Mr. Royall? His girlfriend?"

"She's his assistant. Sticks to him like glue," Louisa said with a rather disapproving sniff. "What do you think of her? *I* think she's kind of snooty."

"Mmm, kind of," Charlotte agreed thoughtfully. Didi Talbot just didn't seem like the typical engineer's assistant, and that aroused her curiosity. "Why do you suppose she stays so close to him? Do you think they're romantically involved? Are they—"

"If you're asking if they share a room, the answer's no. I've had to make both their beds every morning since they came here. But I have heard her going back to her room a couple of times in the middle of the night. Don't know if she's been with him or not. It's not my business."

"No, of course not," Charlotte murmured, somewhat ashamed of succumbing to curiosity. Matt Royall's personal life was no concern of hers, and she was relieved when Louisa ended their conversation by saying it was time to serve dinner.

Since Louisa always dined with guests in her lodge, she and Charlotte joined Matt and Didi at the antique oak table in the dining room. As she sat down, Charlotte noticed with some amusement that the brunette pressed her coral-glossed lips tightly together, apparently considering their presence an intrusion. Her subsequent attempts to exclude them from conversation weren't successful. Whenever she began to drone on about a topic only she and Matt could discuss, he would adroitly change the subject to something more general and draw Louisa and Charlotte into the conversation.

At least he had decent manners, which was more than could be said for his companion, Charlotte thought, looking at him often throughout the meal, trying in vain to assess his personality. Sometimes she sensed a ruthlessness in him, and would decide he was indeed as cold and emotionless as she had suspected. But then, without warning, an easy smile would gentle his carved features, and she would imagine she detected a genuine glimmer of friendliness in his magnificent eyes. He confused her. For that reason she was relieved when dinner ended. Tired of dreading the discussion she had to have with him, she was eager to simply get on with it.

While Louisa began tidying the kitchen, Charlotte carried coffee to Matt and Didi in the public room. After serving them both, she placed the tray on the low table in front of the sofa where they sat together and positioned herself on the edge of a leather chair across from them.

"Could we talk about the airport now?" she asked softly, meeting Matt's penetrating gaze. "It seems like a very good time to—"

"I beg your pardon, it's a terrible time," Didi interrupted haughtily, then turned toward Matt. "Remember? You promised we'd drive over to Steamboat Springs tonight where they at least have a little nightlife. I feel like I've been cooped up in this lodge for ages. I really do want to go somewhere."

Matt's expression remained inscrutable, but he did incline his head in a brief nod. He looked at Charlotte again. "It seems I have a prior commitment. Can we have our talk tomorrow?"

"Fine. When?" she asked stiffly, scarcely able to conceal her impatience as every muscle in her slender body seemed to tense. Determination gleamed in her green eyes but she managed to sound innocently inquiring as she added, "Can we set a definite time?"

"I'll be away from the lodge all day. How about after dinner tomorrow evening?" he suggested, then smiled faintly. "I see no reason to set up a formal appointment. I'm more than willing to talk to you at the first available opportunity."

"I'm glad to hear it," Charlotte replied, rising lithely to her feet to look down at him, her gaze serious. "You know how important it is for me to talk to you. Please don't put me off again . . . for Aunt Lou's sake. Now, if you'll both excuse me, I'll go help her in the kitchen. Have a nice evening in Steamboat Springs. If you've never been there, I'd suggest a little place called Maxine's. It's a very nice tavern."

"Would you like to join us, Charlotte?" he asked as she started to walk away. Ignoring Didi's soft gasp of dismay, he looked up at Charlotte, his eyes traveling slowly over her and almost seeming to glint with amusement when he saw the surprise on her face. "We'd be happy to have you."

"You're kind to ask me, but no thank you. I want to stay with Aunt Lou since it's my first night here," she answered softly, completely baffled by his unexpected invitation. With a somewhat uncertain smile, she excused herself again and went back into the kitchen, wondering if everyone found Matt Royall as puzzling as she did.

After a quiet evening of conversation, Louisa retired about nine thirty. Charlotte remained downstairs another hour, waiting for the flames in the fireplace to die down to glowing embers. After spreading the hot ashes with a poker, she closed the wire-mesh screen over the fireplace and went upstairs, looking forward to a long relaxing soak in the tub in the bathroom she and her aunt shared. For thirty minutes she luxuriated in the feel of hot scented water caressing her skin, and a pleasant drowsiness stole over her. Yet when she got

41

into bed later, snuggling beneath the covers, the events of the day replayed themselves in her memory.

Worrisome thoughts chased each other through her mind, and she began to dwell on her aunt's frail appearance. It was as if she had aged several years since Charlotte had last seen her, and it seemed that the shortness of breath she had exhibited for several years had now worsened. Obviously the concern about the airport was having an adverse effect on Louisa's heart condition. Charlotte shifted restlessly in her bed, a horrid feeling of impotence growing in her as she realized she had made absolutely no progress today to help her aunt.

Two hours later Charlotte was still awake, frustration mounting as her tossing and turning continued. Finally she sat up and tossed the covers back. Knowing very well that lying awake all night was not going to help her aunt, she decided to go down to the kitchen in the hope that a glass of warm milk would induce sleepiness.

Swinging her legs over the side of the bed, she felt for her slippers, found them, and slid them onto her small feet. She stood up, but as she was tying her robe snugly around her waist, the muffled sound of car doors closing elicited an exasperated sigh, and she sank back down on the edge of the bed again. This just didn't seem to be her night. Now she had to wait until Matt and Didi came up to their rooms before she could go down to the kitchen, because she had no desire to run into either of them. Poised on the bed, she shivered. October in the mountains brought chilling nights, and she briskly rubbed her hands over her arms to create a warming friction.

A few minutes later, after Matt and Didi came up-stairs, Charlotte tiptoed out of her room, along the hall, and down to the kitchen. The light of a full moon shone in through the windows, providing enough illumination for Charlotte to take a saucepan from a lower cabinet and the milk from the refrigerator. Several minutes later the warmth of the milk began radiating through her and the need to rest made her eyelids grow heavy. A blessed drowsiness stole over her, but she decided to wash the saucepan and her glass before going to bed again. She took them to the sink, and unable to see clearly in the dim light, banged the pan against the faucet. Though the noise reverberated in the spacious kitchen, she doubted it had been loud enough to disturb anyone upstairs. She proceeded to wash and dry the dishes, then jumped when the kitchen light suddenly flared on. Her heart lurched, beating frantically, and its pace didn't slow when she spun around and found Matt Royall standing in the doorway. Shirtless, his trousers slung low on his lean hips, he was regarding her intently, his eyes flicking over her from head to foot.

"Good heavens! You nearly scared me to death," Charlotte said breathlessly, laying a hand on her chest. "I didn't hear you."

"I could say the same for you. I didn't hear you come downstairs earlier either," he replied, his deep voice lowered to a pleasant roughness. "When I heard a noise down here, I decided to investigate."

"I'm sorry I disturbed you," Charlotte murmured, unconsciously clasping the lapels of her robe together. His sheer size seemed to diminish the room. His tall body effectively blocked the doorway, and she walked toward him with some reluctance. "I was about to go back to bed."

Silently he moved aside, holding the door open for her as she preceded him. They walked together to the stairs and he still said nothing, until Charlotte lifted the hem of her robe to take the first step.

"Are you so worried about your aunt that you couldn't sleep?" he asked softly, lightly catching her arm to turn her around to face him. When the unexpected gesture nearly made her lose her balance, his hands spanned her waist, holding her steady while his darkening gaze played over her tousled gold hair and delicate features. "It's obvious she means a great deal to you. It had to be inconvenient for you to drop everything and get time off from work to come up here."

"Luckily, free-lance commercial artists can work almost anywhere," Charlotte answered, striving to keep her voice steady although she was suddenly far too aware of Matt as an attractive man. The soft light burning at the top of the stairs glinted in his sandy hair and glimmered on bronzed skin. His nearness was disconcerting, and there was something oddly intimate about standing there with him in the middle of the night. She began to wish one of them at least was fully dressed. Elevated as she was by the first step, her face was almost on a level with his, so she had no choice except to look directly at him as she continued, "But even if I did have a regular job, I'd have come up here anyway. Aunt Lou needs me. She's a special person. That's why I'm so anxious to talk to you about the airport."

He nodded. "I understand that. Frankly, I'm a little surprised you aren't insisting we discuss the problem

44

right now, since we're alone and it's unlikely we'd be interrupted."

"Oh, but it's after one. I wouldn't expect you to want to talk now," Charlotte explained, then smiled rather sheepishly. "I might *wish* you'd talk to me, but I know you must be tired and you have to work tomorrow. This just isn't the right time."

His answering smile was gentle as he said softly, "A woman with a really good sense of timing is hard to find."

Cool and brusque and businesslike, he was compelling enough, but in this gentle teasing mood he was irresistibly magnetic. Suddenly the warmth of his long fingers curved into the small of her back, penetrating the cotton of her robe and gown as if he were touching bare skin. Though astounded by the rush of sensual awareness that swept over her, Charlotte managed to conceal her true response behind a nonchalant smile. Yet when he began to draw her slowly toward him, her breathing ceased and instinct brought her hands up against his bare chest. His hair-roughened skin was warm beneath her fingers, and she had to fight a nearly overpowering desire to trace her fingertips over his muscles. She tensed when he reached up with one hand and brushed the ball of his thumb over the slender length of her neck, seeking and finding the rapidly beating pulse there.

"Your heart's pounding," he whispered, the glinting flame that appeared in his eyes burning into the lambent depths of hers. His fingertips feathered gently down to the low vee of her robe. "Pounding, Charlotte . . . surely not simply because I startled you in the kitchen?"

"It's late," she said, catching his wandering fingers in her own before the incredible weakness invading her lower limbs could intensify. "Very late, Mr. Royall."

"Matt," he amended huskily. "Mr. Royall is far too formal."

Charlotte nodded, unable to move, though she knew she should. "First names are friendlier," she agreed, sounding far more composed than she felt. And when Matt unexpectedly slipped his arm completely around her waist and caught her chin between the thumb and forefinger of his free hand, tilting her head back slightly, she had to bite back a startled gasp. "Matt . . ."

"What a lovely little wood nymph you are. How's a man supposed to resist you in the middle of the night?" he whispered, then brought her closer to his body, his mouth seeking and finding hers.

His kiss was electric, warm, and demanding even in the initial gentleness. But when her mouth opened slightly with her swift intake of breath, the kiss deepened, became a devouring possession. Matt was the aggressor, and for a few insane moments Charlotte surrendered to the tide of responsive passion that throbbed through her veins. Her hands went up to brush over smooth muscled shoulders, but as Matt whispered her name, the reality of what she was doing hit her. With a murmured protest, she moved away from him, up to the next step.

"Good night, Matt," she murmured, hoping he couldn't recognize the disruptive effect the past minute or so had had on her senses. "I'll see you in the morning."

"Matt, do you know how terribly late it is?" Didi suddenly called down as she leaned over the railing above them. "Aren't you ever coming upstairs?"

"I plan to," he replied dryly, but his gaze never left Charlotte as she looked up quickly and saw the semi-transparent aqua negligee the older woman was wearing. When she turned back to him again with a slightly sardonic smile, he met her cool stare.

"Good night again," she said crisply.

Charlotte slowly ascended the steps, nodded perfunctorily at Didi, then continued on to her room without a backward glance. After closing her door firmly behind her, she went straight to bed, curling up in the center of the mattress and wrapping her arms around her fat pillow. She touched trembling fingertips to the lips Matt had just so thoroughly kissed and closed her eyes. Matt no longer seemed such a mystery. Though he had nearly convinced her tonight that he was capable of warmth, she wasn't sure now. Certainly only a cold man could passionately kiss one woman while another awaited him in his bed. It was a pity. Matt was attractive, intelligent, magnetically sensuous. Charlotte knew that for a few minutes she had felt intensely drawn to him, but the last thing in the world she needed was to become involved with a man who wasn't warm and caring.

CHAPTER THREE

Charlotte spent the next morning helping her aunt in the lodge. After lunch, when Louisa went to her room for an afternoon rest, Charlotte put on her hiking boots and took her sketchbook out into the woods. Breathing in the crisp autumn air, she lifted her face occasionally to the warming rays of the sun and marveled at the vibrant blue sky, dotted here and there with fluffy white clouds. She walked along the bank of the rollicking brook, fallen leaves crunching beneath her feet. All around her the slopes were blanketed in brilliant oranges and reds and softer yellows, and with every gentle breeze, increasing numbers of leaves floated slowly to the ground. Boughs of the slender aspens swayed and showered her with rustling golden leaves as she walked through a small thicket where the brook meandered.

The hardiest of the birds, those that never flew south, chirped merrily from high branches, apparently undaunted by the colder air and brisker winds that heralded winter. Charlotte wasn't surprised to notice so many birds gathering near the lodge, because in fair weather or foul, Aunt Louisa kept several large feeders brimming with seed. Even the deepest of snows didn't prevent her from going out to replenish the suet in the wire baskets attached to tree trunks surrounding the lodge. Yet it wasn't only the birds that Louisa Jordan treasured. Every creature in the woods that was brave enough to venture near the lodge found a treat. For deer, there was a block of salt, and any raccoon that happened by could find a pan of scraps near the back door, put there to keep them out of the rubbish bin, or so Aunt Lou pretended. Because of her concern, a veritable menagerie of animals frequented the lodge, especially in winter.

Remembering how often she had teased her aunt by telling her she should get her home declared a wildlife refuge, Charlotte smiled as she walked up a steep slope beside the brook. Her smile became wistful, then faded completely as she considered how damaging an airport on the plateau would be. Its accompanying noise and commotion would frighten most of the birds and animals away, and yet another pleasure would vanish from Aunt Lou's life.

"Damn, it's not fair," she muttered, tucking a wayward strand of hair behind her ear. Frustration began rising in her, then receded as she entered a familiar small clearing and saw the changes the seasons of spring and summer had made. Every time she visited the clearing it seemed more exquisitely pristine. An outcropping of rock overhung the brook, and a thick carpet of pine needles covered the ground. The rock, the brook, and the carpet of needles were the only constants in the scene; new growth was always burgeoning forth, wildflowers in spring and summer along with a number of tree saplings. The wildflowers had faded and dried now, but the new trees remained. Delighting in the beauty, Charlotte approached a small aspen sapling around which four cedars had sprung up, forming such a perfect circle that it seemed they must have been deliberately planted there. It was one of those simple miracles of nature she couldn't resist. Taking a pencil from her jacket pocket, she perched herself as comfortably as possible on the rounded rock and began to sketch.

Engrossed in her work, she was hardly aware that time was passing, until her right leg began to stiffen from being used as an easel for her sketch pad. She extended it gingerly, wincing as prickling sensations jabbed her calf. After flexing her knee several times, the mild discomfort passed. Putting the sketchbook aside, she relaxed, but even as she closed her eyes for a moment, an eerie sensation trickled down her spine, warning her she was being watched. Her eyes flew open and she swiftly looked downstream. Her instinct had been correct. Matt Royall stood at the edge of the clearing, tall and lean and decidedly masculine in a hunter's jacket and fawn-colored corduroy pants. With a weak smile Charlotte lowered her feet to the ground and stood beside the rock.

"Mr. Royall . . . Matt, I didn't hear you—again. How long have you been there?"

"About five minutes," he told her, walking over to her. With a gesture he indicated the sketchbook. "Creating a masterpiece?"

"It's more likely to become a greeting card," she said wryly, trying to suppress the feeling of vulnerability she felt, knowing he had observed her for such a long time. "But even though none of my drawings will ever be considered great works of art, I still enjoy doing them."

"May I see it?" he asked, reaching around her to take the sketchbook off the rock. When she nodded, he flipped back the cover and studied the drawing, stroking his jaw thoughtfully with one finger. After a few moments he moved closer, holding the sketchbook where she could see it, and lightly tapped a knuckle against the shadowed wood that was the drawing's background. "I like the way you've only used a few strokes to create distance here. And the cedars around the aspen are beautiful. I like it, Charlotte."

She thanked him, trying not to sound as unreasonably pleased by his praise as she felt. Taking the sketchbook when he handed it back to her, she hugged it against her chest and smiled questioningly up at him. "I thought you and the crew were still working up on the plateau. What brings you down here? Are you planning to survey this area too?"

He shook his head. "I just felt like taking a walk. When the crew started taking soil samples, I had a few minutes free and decided I'd wander down here."

"Didn't Didi wander down with you?"

"I sent her to pick up some maps at the county seat."

Charlotte leaned back against the rock and gazed out into the woods. "Aunt Lou said Didi is your assistant. Does that mean she has an engineering degree too?"

"No, Didi doesn't really know a great deal about engineering. She runs errands mostly." Twirling a slender stalk of dried grass between his fingers, Matt smiled faintly. "Actually, her father is my partner, and he wanted to manufacture this job for her so she'd have some work experience."

The situation sounded unpleasantly familiar, and with an involuntary twist of her lips, Charlotte thought about Brad and how willing he was to try to advance his career by romancing his boss's daughter. Was Matt the same kind of man? Didi's presence seemed to indicate he was. Why would he let Didi tag along on projects with him, doing a manufactured job, unless the arrangement was in some way advantageous to him? Charlotte was sorely tempted to ask him, but decided she might very well be told it was none of her business. With a mere nod, she acknowledged his explanation.

"I noticed this morning that your aunt seems much happier since you arrived. How long do you plan to stay with her?"

"As long as she needs me," Charlotte replied without hesitation, then turned her head to look up at him, something akin to suspicion darkening her eyes. "Why do you ask?"

He met her questioning gaze directly, and his answer was blunt and frightening. "She just may need you a great deal during the next few weeks."

"What are you saying exactly?" Charlotte asked, her voice strained. "Have you already made a decision, like Commissioner Fletcher implied yesterday afternoon? Are you really going to locate the airport on the plateau?"

"No decision has been made, no matter what Fletcher said," Matt replied, suddenly reaching out to grip her shoulders and squeeze them firmly, as if to lend credence to his denial. A combination of impatience and regret flickered across his face and hardened his jaw. "Surveys on the other potential sites haven't been completed yet, and until they're all done, no decision will be made." His voice was gentle as he said, "But I think you should know the truth, Charlotte. From simply walking over the sites, and from the data we've already gathered, I suspect the plateau will be the most logical location."

"I don't see why! I don't understand why you have to even consider it as a possible site," Charlotte said urgently, hardly aware that she lightly clasped the lapels of his coat, and completely unaware of the plea that softened her emerald eyes. "Really, Matt, why can't you just cross the plateau off your list? I don't see why it would matter if you did. There must be half a dozen other plateaus in this county that could be used for the airport."

"And three of them are located in federally protected forests. That eliminates them automatically," Matt calmly explained, though his narrowed gaze conveyed understanding. "With only three other potential sites left to consider, I couldn't possibly just cross one off the list. I'm sorry, but that's the way it is, the way it has to be."

"Doesn't Aunt Lou have any rights in this situation? Doesn't anybody care about her feelings? She's lived in that lodge for so many years that it's almost become her life, especially since my great-uncle Will died." Charlotte stepped closer to Matt, her entire body trembling in her determination to make him understand her aunt's plight. "Let me just tell you what her home means to her. Will you listen?"

Sighing, he nodded. "I'll listen. But Charlotte, you should know that—"

Pressing fingertips against his lips, she halted his words and whispered beseechingly, "Please, let me tell you everything. Let me make you understand exactly how she's feeling right now, when her very way of life is being threatened."

The story began to tumble from her, and to her relief, Matt was completely attentive, even showing signs of genuine sympathy as she told him about Louisa's love of the wildlife, about the pleasure she gained from the guests who frequented her lodge, guests who probably wouldn't return if a nearby airport displaced the seclusion they sought. "And there's something you couldn't possibly know," she finished. "Aunt Lou has made the lodge and the land around it a memorial for Uncle Will. They never had any children; they could only share a way of life that both of them adored. Aside from memories, this land is all Aunt Lou has left of him. Moving somewhere else wouldn't be right. You can't want to take that away from her."

A muscle ticked in Matt's clenched jaw. "I don't want to take anything from your aunt. I like her; I respect her. But—"

"She's getting on in years. Why can't she live the time she has left in peace?" Charlotte persisted. "If you decided not to consider the plateau and I could tell her she no longer has to worry about—"

"Charlotte, that's not possible," he interrupted grimly, taking her small hands in his. "Be reasonable."

"She has a heart condition, Matt. I'm sure she's

never told you that. But I can tell you that it's gotten worse since this mess started."

"I wish I could do something to make everything different, but it's out of my hands. The majority of people in this county want an airport. If it's decided that the plateau is the best possible site, your aunt will be placed in the unlucky position of having to make the sacrifice. It's no one's fault that her lodge happens to be located nearby. She's certainly not the first person to be involved in this kind of situation. Sometimes people sell their homes and move to make way for a road or a hospital or whatever. I know it doesn't seem fair, but it happens."

Charlotte slipped her hands from his and stuffed them into the pockets of her jacket. Looking up at Matt, she shook her head. "I'm afraid I can't view the situation as emotionlessly as you do. How can you be so cold? You know Aunt Lou, but you seem to be saying that hard facts are all that matter in this situation. But what about feelings? Or don't you have any?"

"Charlotte, be careful," he warned, impatience glittering in his eyes. "I know how frustrated you must be feeling right now, but—"

"If I could only make you understand what a wonderful woman Aunt Lou is," Charlotte said, her voice wavering. Her chin wobbled slightly and a tear spilled over, catching in the thick fringe of her lower lashes.

"For God's sake," Matt muttered, pulling her hands from her pockets while drawing her to him. "Charlotte, don't cry."

"I'm not crying," she mumbled, tensing at first, then succumbing to the large hands that moved in comforting strokes down her back. Her head came to rest in the hollow of his neck and she allowed herself to relax, though her hands were still planted firmly against his chest. Unwilling to show any further signs of weakness, she blinked back tears until her eyes were dry again. She took a deep tremulous breath. "It's just that all this is making Aunt Lou so unhappy, and no one seems to care except me."

Without a word Matt tilted her chin up and brushed away the tear from her lashes with a gentle fingertip. The kiss he brushed against her forehead was like one he might give a hurt child, yet when he lifted his head and Charlotte's eyes flickered open to look up into the amber depths of his, everything was suddenly different. An intense silence surrounded them. Even the breeze stilled. And as they looked at each other for several long moments, Charlotte's senses awoke to a keener awareness and her breath caught when a warning glow of desire flared in his eyes. The warmth of his body seemed to envelop her, and she detected the spicy scent of his after-shave. As if mesmerized, she was unable to protest when the edge of his thumb pressed lightly into her chin, tugging her lips apart. His intent was obvious, yet she was powerless, incapable of struggle when he lowered his head and trailed a strand of burning kisses across her cheek, toward her mouth. Her heart began to thud rapidly as anticipation mounted, then his mouth touched her own and her senses spiraled. Had he been rough, she might have been able to fight him. But his firm lips played over hers, teasing, coaxing, tormenting her by releasing her completely and making her await another kiss.

Strong even teeth nibbled the fullness of her lower

lip, sending tremors of delight down her spine. Her breath began to come in soft little gasps, mingling with the minty warmth of his, and when he had brought her to the point where she needed a real kiss from him, his mouth possessed hers completely. His long fingers slipped into her silky hair and he cupped the back of her head in one hand, holding her still. His other hand encircled her waist, drawing her close. As her tender curves yielded to the enticingly firm contours of his body, her hands feathered up to the sun-browned column of his neck, her fingertips eagerly tracing strong tendons. With her touch, his lips exerted an increasing pressure that gently twisted her own, and with her breathless whispering of his name, her mouth opened invitingly beneath his.

It was as if no one else in the world existed except the two of them. A rushing of warmth surged through Charlotte, draining strength from her legs. She actually felt dizzy, caught up in pure sensual pleasure. His heated flesh seemed to sear her skin even through their clothing, and when the hand cupping her nape tilted her head back, and his mouth sought the creamy smoothness of her neck, a shattering thrill shot through her. She couldn't resist when he undid the top three buttons of her blouse, then trailed searching kisses downward. She trembled when the tip of his tongue tasted the scented hollow between her breasts.

Matt pulled her closer, and when she felt his aroused masculinity against her, she came to her senses with a jolt. Stiffening, Charlotte pushed against his chest and moved away from him the moment he reluctantly released her. Smoothing her tousled hair, she tried valiantly to regain some semblance of composure, no easy accomplishment, especially when she met the fiery glint of his narrowed gaze.

"You see, Charlotte," he said unevenly, "I am capable of feeling."

"I never imagined for a moment you weren't capable of passion," she replied, confusion about her ardent response to him making her defensive. "But I also know that passion isn't the same thing as compassion."

"What an astute observation. But don't you think you're making a snap judgment about my character? You can't possibly know what I'm really like."

"I know you well enough to realize you care more about facts and figures than you do about people," she declared recklessly. "You practically said so yourself."

"No, you jumped to that conclusion simply because I tried to explain some of the painful realities of life to you. I never told you that I don't care how your aunt feels right now. I know she's worried and I also know she could be hurt badly in this situation. Believe me, that bothers me."

"Then why can't you just cross the plateau off your list of potential sites?" Charlotte exclaimed. "You'd be making an elderly lady's last years happy, and the county would still get its airport, just in another location."

"Charlotte, you're grasping at straws and I think you know it," Matt said as he moved toward her. "You're an intelligent woman. You realize that I couldn't possibly do what you're asking. I'm being paid by the citizens of this county to build an airport, and I'd be shirking my responsibilities if I didn't consider all the potential sites, then chose the best one.

That may or may not be the plateau behind your aunt's lodge. We'll simply have to wait until all the surveys are completed and studied before we know for certain."

Deep inside she grasped the logic of what he was saying, but stubborn pride and the gnawing concern she felt for her aunt wouldn't allow her to admit that to him. Besides, desperation had made her willing to ask the impossible of him, in the slimmest hope that he might give it. But now even desperate measures had failed, and she felt her wisest course of action at the moment was to simply walk away. Proudly lifting her chin, she started to move around him. Her heart seemed to leap up into her throat when he caught her wrist, stopping her before she had taken a second step.

"Don't try to find someone to blame," he cautioned. "This is one of those unfortunate situations where no one is at fault."

"I'll be sure to tell Aunt Lou that. No doubt it will make her feel better."

"Don't try me too far, Charlotte," he warned gruffly, something unidentifiable flaring in his eyes. "There's a limit to my patience, and you're coming close to overstepping the mark."

"Then kindly let go of me and I'll take myself right out of your sight," she retorted, her cool expression concealing myriad seething emotions.

Relief washed over her when he released her wrist. She managed to stroll nonchalantly out of the clearing and along the brook, her shoulders resolutely squared until she knew she was out of his sight. She slowed her pace then, and raking her fingers through her hair, gave a tremulous sigh.

Matt Royall was not going to help Aunt Lou, Charlotte thought, and she had been foolish all along to foster any hope that he might. Then, to her eternal shame, she had compounded her foolishness by responding so ardently to his kisses—responded to the very man who wouldn't hesitate to break her aunt's heart! She could never allow that to happen again. Yet even as she determined to exercise more control, she was honest enough with herself to admit that she was more physically attracted to Matt than she had ever been to any other man in her life, including Brad. And Matt was certainly no novice in the art of seduction. Even now, as she recalled the power of his mouth and the tantalizing sensitivity of his hands wandering over her, an unbidden thrill rushed through her, causing her breath to catch. She caught her lower lip between her teeth and sighed. No doubt about it—Matt was a dangerous man. For her own good, she knew she had to stay away from him.

Charlotte did steer clear of Matt as much as possible during the next two days, and he seemed to like it that way. They spoke politely to each other, if necessary, but when they had to dine together in the evenings, Charlotte felt the tension between them was almost tangible. On occasion, when she cast a surreptitious glance in his direction, she would find him watching her, the expression in his hooded eyes unreadable, yet disturbing nonetheless. Was he recalling her passionate response to him in the clearing? she wondered, unable to prevent every inch of her skin from burning at the memory. Or was he merely feeling scorn for what he considered her overly emotional compulsion to protect her aunt? Charlotte was inclined to believe that it was disdain he felt.

Despite the fact that Matt's presence in the lodge still disturbed her, she tried her best not to think about him. Since it was obvious he intended to do nothing to aid Aunt Lou, Charlotte felt she needed to search for some other ally. But who? Commissioner Fletcher was hardly a likely candidate, but she thought it might be worth approaching some of the other members of the commission, whose names Mayor Kelly could give her.

Charlotte was thinking about it after dinner Wednesday evening, while she removed the antique cloth from the dining room table. With a silent prayer that at least one commission member would feel some compassion for Aunt Lou, she carefully folded the cloth and stored it away in the lower cabinet of the oak hutch. Out of the corner of her eye she saw a shadow fall across the polished floor. She turned toward the doorway, and to her dismay her heart did a crazy somersault when Matt stepped up to the table, directly across from her.

"I want to talk to you, Charlotte," he stated, his low voice firm, yet not curt, as it sometimes was. "I have a proposition for you."

"Proposition? What—"

"Let's sit down," he commanded, rather than suggested, waving her into the chair she stood behind while pulling out the one before him. When they were seated, he immediately came to the point. "The draftsman with my crew broke his arm this afternoon. After it was set by the local doctor, one of the other men drove him home to Denver. In other words, I'm without a draftsman now, and our Denver office told me it might be two or three weeks before they can hire a replacement to send up here." Extending both arms out on the tabletop, palms down, he strummed the fingers of one hand as piercing tiger eyes held hers. "I was hoping maybe you could help me out. Have you ever taken a course in mechanical drawing?"

Total astonishment struck her dumb for a moment, but she finally untangled her tongue. "Well, yes, I did, but . . . I'm no draftsman."

"I wouldn't need you to do actual working drawings. It's early in the project—all specifics aren't necessary yet," he explained. "What I'd want from you would be basic site sketches. I'd do rough drafts, including the general information: elevations, precise measurements, pertinent geological information. Then you'd draw to scale. I'm sure you could do it."

Amazed that he was really suggesting she work for him, she slowly shook her head. "I don't know. It's been a long time since I did any mechanical drawing. I'm not sure I could do it."

"I bet you can, at least to satisfy my present need. And the work wouldn't be very time consuming. Except for visiting each site once, you could do the work right here. I'll have the drafting equipment moved to the lodge from the trailer where our draftsman worked. If you have any trouble, which I doubt, I'll help you. But you'll have plenty of time to fulfill your obligations to your clients because I really only need one basic sketch of each potential site to present to the county commissioners."

Convinced by now that he was serious, Charlotte felt growing resentment. How dare he offer her money to become involved in a project that might very well disrupt her aunt's life! Clenching her hands tightly together in her lap, she met his direct gaze unflinchingly and shook her head. "Maybe I could do the work, but I have to refuse your offer. I'd feel like a traitor if I did anything to help this project along, considering the fact that the end result might ruin Aunt Lou's life."

"Ah, Charlotte, what a loyal little thing you are," he said softly, a somewhat indulgent quirk tugging up one corner of his mouth. His eyes narrowed, accentuating the carved contours of his face. "But I'm not the enemy. If you help me, you'll really be helping Louisa too. If I have to do these scale drawings myself, that's going to prolong the time it takes to evaluate all the sites, and the longer it takes for the final decision to be made, the more your aunt's worries will increase."

Swamped by sudden indecision, Charlotte thought about it. What Matt said made sense—waiting for the decision would worry Aunt Lou to distraction. So if she could do anything to shorten that waiting time, she should do it. Still, there were other considerations that made her more than hesitant. Did she dare put herself into a position where she might be working closely with Matt? After what had happened between them up in the clearing, it might be extremely foolish for her to be with him any more than she had to be. Yet she was an adult, she told herself sternly. Surely she could control her physical attraction to him. Especially if working for him benefited her aunt. Wavering, but still unsure how she should answer him, she spread her hands, palms upward, in a gesture of uncertainty.

"I don't know what to say," she admitted softly.

"Besides, you're not even sure I can do the work properly."

"I'm prepared to find out," he said, smiling faintly.

Matt went around the table, pulled out her chair, and she automatically rose to her feet. His hand rested against the small of her back as he escorted her into the public room. At the rolltop desk in one corner, he pulled the chair out and indicated with a gesture for her to take a seat. She did, but a puzzled frown marred her brow. Her confusion vanished, however, when Matt extracted a map from a protective cardboard cylinder, smoothing it open on the desk before her.

"A contour map? Oh dear, I've only done a couple of those in my life," Charlotte admitted with a grimace. "And that was a long time ago, when I took mechanical drawing in college."

"At your age it couldn't possibly have been 'a long time ago,'" he replied dryly. Laying one arm over the back of her chair, he leaned down, his face disturbingly close to her own as he ran a finger across the map. "I'm sure you remember how the grade of the land is represented by these curved lines, and that the numbers between them represent elevations."

She could only nod. Too aware suddenly of his faint evocative scent, she didn't completely trust herself to speak without sounding revealingly breathless. He had the power to do that to her—make her feel breathless simply by moving within touching distance. Charlotte was nearly overcome by an incredible desire to stroke a fingertip along the strong line of his jaw, a desire she hastily suppressed. This close to him, she was able to detect the barely discernible stubble of a day's growth of his beard, which merely served to enhance his already compelling virility. Suddenly caught up in the memory of the kiss they had shared, she found it difficult to concentrate completely on what he was saying, but sheer willpower came to the rescue. She arranged her face into composed lines and watched him attentively, determined not to allow her gaze to drift down to the attractive V of suntanned skin exposed at his open shirt collar.

"All the terms sound familiar, don't they?" he finished, looking directly at her as she nodded. "Well then, there's no problem. I won't expect you to do anything more complex than this. And I'll be here to help you if you have trouble. How would you prefer to be paid, by the hour or with a set fee for each drawing?"

Unable to drag her gaze away from his, feeling his breath fan her warm cheeks, Charlotte wished he wasn't leaning so close. Such proximity wasn't conducive to rational thought. "I really hadn't thought about it," she answered at last. "Actually, I haven't even agreed to do the work yet."

"But you're going to," he stated confidently, his amber eyes boring into hers. "Aren't you?"

Common sense told her to say no immediately, but the desire to get this ordeal over as quickly as possible for her aunt had to be considered. And there was something else—that age-old irresistible pull toward the forbidden; in this instance, Matt Royall. She knew she should stay away from him. She sighed. "All right, I guess I'll do it. But I really need time for my other work. My best client likes to get three to four greeting card designs a month from me."

He nodded. "Like your drawing of the clearing?" he

asked softly, mercifully straightening to look down at her from his considerable height. "You had a good start. Have you finished it yet?"

"Almost." Standing, Charlotte had to fight an intense urge to take a step away from him. He moved closer, and her eyes widened slightly as he reached out to tighten one side tie of her forest green corduroy jumper. His hard knuckles grazed her slender shoulder and set her pulses pounding, but she willed herself to show no visible reaction to his gesture.

An enigmatic half smile curved his lips as he murmured, "It was coming undone."

"Thank you." Brushing a tendril of hair back from one temple, she managed to smile quite serenely up at him, though he was looking at her so intently that she got the vague impression he was about to say something more. If he had intended to, he never had the chance. At that moment Didi Talbot walked down the stairs. Every strand of her dark hair was in place, and she was wearing a beautifully tailored tweed skirt, a silk blouse, and low-heeled pumps.

Didi seemed displeased to find Charlotte with Matt. She barely inclined her head in a greeting, then clasped her hands around his arm, as if staking claim to him.

"Charlotte's going to help with the site drawings until we can get another draftsman up here," Matt announced, moving out of Didi's tenacious grasp to roll up the map and slip it back into its cylinder. He gave Charlotte a warm smile. "She'll save us a great deal of time."

Didi didn't act impressed. In fact, Charlotte thought she practically stared a hole through her while Matt had his back to them. Working with Didi promised to be a barrel of laughs, Charlotte mused, then realized the older woman might turn out to be a blessing in disguise. Her presence virtually assured that Charlotte wouldn't often be alone with Matt. It also served as a reminder that a few kisses from Matt probably didn't mean anything to him. Charlotte sighed. What was she getting herself into?

CHAPTER FOUR

Charlotte was downstairs by seven thirty Saturday morning. Clad in sturdy wool slacks, a warm sweater, and thick socks inside her hiking boots, she tossed her down-filled parka across the back of the sofa in the public room. She was waiting for Matt to come down. Though he didn't require his crew to work on weekends, he had told Charlotte he wanted her to see the next site he intended to survey. She didn't mind giving up her Saturday morning. In fact, she was eager to see any site that might prove more suitable than the plateau for the airport.

Hearing her aunt moving around in the kitchen, Charlotte started in that direction then stopped when Matt loped easily down the stairs. His navy crewneck sweater covered a light blue shirt, and the faded denim of his jeans stretched tautly over his thighs with every long stride. Looking up, he saw Charlotte watching and smiled approvingly.

"Ready to go, I see. And it's only a minute past seven. I must say it's a pleasure to find a woman who knows how to be punctual."

"I'll pretend that comment didn't sound the least bit chauvinistic," Charlotte said with mock solemnity.

"I wasn't criticizing women in general," he replied, amusement evident in his tone. "Maybe I've just worked with Didi too long. Unless I crack the whip, she's late for everything."

And she's late again right now, Charlotte thought, not at all surprised. Matt had been able to coerce Didi to be on time during the week, but this was Saturday, and apparently she was still lingering before her mirror. She spent an unreasonable amount of time grooming herself, almost as if it were a compulsion. In the week Charlotte had been at the lodge, she had noticed that it took at least an hour, usually longer, for Didi to make herself presentable for dinner. And if she decided to dawdle upstairs that long this morning, she would undoubtedly keep them waiting.

Charlotte watched as Matt paused at the bottom of the stairs, one booted foot propped up on the first riser as he jotted something down in the small note pad he held in his left hand. Once again she realized with a start how attractive he was, and she felt an absurd need to run her fingers through his thick sandy hair. Such needs were coming over her more frequently now, and she was often disgusted with herself for becoming so caught up in simple physical attraction to a man. It was uncharacteristic for her, but she told herself that everyone was entitled to occasional lapses of good sense—as long as those lapses didn't evolve into habits.

Now, as he turned toward her, she pushed all such fanciful notions aside. Concentrating on more practical matters, she excused herself to go help her aunt in the kitchen. Fifteen minutes later, as Matt was sitting down to breakfast, Charlotte hovered uncertainly by his chair after pouring a cup of coffee for him. Didi was still not downstairs.

"Should I go see what's keeping Didi?" she asked. "I know you wanted to get an early start."

"Didi decided late last night that she had to go back to Denver for a friend's engagement party this evening. She rode back with some of the crew about five this morning." Matt smiled wryly. "She was horrified at the thought of having to be ready to go anywhere at such an 'ungodly hour,' but since I said I couldn't drive her back today, she had no choice. And she had to go in the truck—not her favorite form of transportation."

"Can't say I'm surprised she went," Louisa commented, smiling thanks at Charlotte, who poured her coffee too. "While you two were going over those maps last night, she told me this was the most boring place she'd ever been in her life. 'Nothing to do.' She must've said that at least a dozen times."

Didi had never acted all that bored before, Charlotte thought after filling her own cup and sitting down. But then, Matt hadn't been as attentive to Didi the past couple of days. Thursday and Friday evenings he had gone over contour maps and site sketches with Charlotte so she could become more familiar with them before attempting to do one herself. Naturally Didi hadn't liked playing second fiddle, even temporarily, but Charlotte was surprised she'd actually gone to Denver for the weekend. But she had, and that meant Charlotte and Matt would be visiting the site alone today. And tonight, after Louisa went to bed, they would be alone again. That realization was enough to quicken her breathing. Yet there was nothing to be done about the situation now, and Charlotte was determined not to succumb to an exaggerated fear of being alone with him.

Shortly after breakfast Matt and Charlotte left in the Jeep. After passing through Royal View, Matt turned north onto a narrow road that wound over rocky hills overshadowed by higher snowcapped peaks. As their journey extended, Charlotte realized they were fast approaching the state line where Colorado bordered Wyoming, and her heart sank lower with every mile that took them farther from the center of the county. Despite her prejudice, she knew it only made sense for a county airport to be centrally located. She only hoped that the site they were about to visit would compensate for its location by being perfect for an airport in every other way.

Wondering what Matt was thinking, she gave him a quick glance, but his carved profile told her nothing except that he seemed to be concentrating on negotiating the tight curves of the road. Turning to gaze out her window again, Charlotte was awed by their surroundings. Even the old scars left here and there on the mountainsides by abandoned silver mines were beginning to fade, concealed by undergrowth and trees that were reclaiming the land. It was hard to imagine that ore cars had once disturbed the pristine silence with their clatter. Now peace reigned on the hillsides again, and some of Charlotte's tension began slipping away.

When Matt slowed the Jeep a few minutes later and pulled off the road onto an overlook, Charlotte drew in a swift breath at the exquisite scene stretched out below. She eagerly extended a hand to Matt when he

got out and came around to open her door. With unbridled enthusiasm, she hurried to the safety railing.

"I've never been here before. Oh, what a magnificent view," she whispered, looking out across a narrow valley. On the other side, at the base of a series of
rolling hills, a meadow of dried grasses was edged by a
stretch of a rocky creek. With a hand she shaded her
eyes from the glare of the sun, and soon sighted a
house nestled in a grove of aspens that bordered the
meadow. "What a lovely place to live."

"Mmm, lovely," Matt murmured close behind her,
but it wasn't clear if he meant the house or her. His
hands came down lightly on Charlotte's shoulders as
he added, "The meadow's the site we've come to see."

"Really?" Charlotte's hopes soared. The meadow
seemed the perfect site for an airstrip. Before she could
voice that precipitate opinion, Matt turned her back
toward the Jeep and they were on their way again.

The serpentine road took them down from the
heights, past the point where two mountain streams
converged into the wider creek that bordered the
meadow. After going about half a mile, Matt turned
off the highway onto a lane that dipped down to a
narrow wooden bridge that traversed the creek. Obviously a private drive, the lane swung toward the aspens and the gray stone house situated there. Though
it was not quite as large as Louisa's lodge, the two-
story structure possessed a stately elegance. Boxwood
hedges rimmed the grounds, but the foliage had been
clipped away at intervals to form arched entrances.
Through one of the openings Charlotte glimpsed a
neatly arranged rock garden behind the house. It was
now barren except for a few lonely cultivated asters.

Matt didn't take the fork in the drive that cut through the hedge between two stone pillars and led to a garage in back. Yet as he slowed the Jeep to a stop, Charlotte still had a good view of the upper level of the house, where windows were securely shuttered.

"No one's here," she commented softly. "Summer residents, I guess."

"This place is more isolated than your aunt's lodge. I wouldn't want to be here when the heavy snows start. You'd be snowbound for most of the winter," Matt explained offhandedly, switching off the engine and pocketing the key. The narrow meadow stretched out on the other side of the lane, and he surveyed the lay of the land for several moments. Then he turned to Charlotte. "Ready?"

Nodding, she opened her door, got out of the Jeep, and went to join him on the other side. They started across the meadow, the dried grasses rustling around their legs, a clean breeze caressing their faces. Even an early October sun was capable of generating considerable warmth, and the chill had gone off the day. Unzipping her parka, Charlotte looked up at the hills that rolled down to the meadow.

"You know, this place sort of reminds me of Vail," she admitted reluctantly. "I suppose an excellent ski resort *could* be developed here, though it would be a shame to put an end to the peace and quiet."

"An airstrip would end the peace and quiet too," Matt reminded her in a quiet voice, looking down at her as they walked. "But I imagine you'd rather see it built here than on the plateau, wouldn't you, Charlotte?"

She was too intrinsically honest to attempt denial.

Besides, she knew he was far too preceptive to believe her even if she did utter such a lie. So she nodded. "To me, any place would be better than the plateau. But it is beautiful here. I'd hate to see it changed."

"Many areas of the county will be changing if the commissioners have their way," said Matt flatly. "Time just doesn't stand still. Everything can't remain the same. We can only hope the developers are wise enough to preserve as much of the natural beauty as they possibly can, which they probably will since the beauty of ski resorts is a large part of their appeal. An airport, unfortunately, is purely functional, and runways have to be tarmac, not grass."

"And they have to be long," Charlotte added with a sweep of her hand. "Although I admit I'm biased, I'm sure this site is longer than the plateau. And probably flatter. In fact, it seems almost perfect for an airport. Don't you think?"

He looked down into her hopeful green eyes and something akin to regret flickered across his dark face. He shook his head. "Not quite perfect," he said softly, catching her hand to lead her up a gentle slope to the edge of the creek. "See how low the banks are? When the snows melt and the rains come—"

"It floods," Charlotte morosely finished for him. "But how often?"

"Several times a year, especially in the spring. An airstrip under water isn't worth much. And, worse, there's the possibility that excessive flooding would erode the earth beneath the runway, causing it to break up in places."

"What about the house? Surely the creek doesn't flood very often or nobody would have built it there."

"Take a look," he commanded gently, putting his hands on her shoulders to turn her toward the house. "It's on higher ground than most of the meadow."

Charlotte did see, and once again her hope plummeted. "And, of course, there's no chance the plateau would ever be flooded," she said almost inaudibly. "Does this mean you're not really seriously considering this site?"

"We wouldn't be here if that were true," Matt answered, his touch impersonal as he massaged the tensed muscles of her shoulders. "Until we have all the data on each site, none of them will be crossed off the list. But I didn't want you getting up false hopes about this place. I thought you should know it has its drawbacks."

She sighed, and turning around to him, gazed up into his clear amber eyes, unaware that a shadow of vulnerability fell across her face. "Well, I'm going to keep hoping anyway. I just have this instinctive feeling that one of the other sites will be more suitable than the plateau."

"Don't let yourself get too caught up in wishful thinking. You have to be realistic or risk—" Matt broke off his cautioning words when she moved away from him, as if she couldn't bear to listen.

For the next half hour they walked the length and breadth of the meadow, exchanging only a few words. Charlotte had erected a barrier between them, and he was showing no inclination to try to break it down. As they followed the creek toward the house, Charlotte decided to shed her jacket. Walking at a fast pace to keep up with Matt's long strides, she felt more comfortable with the parka tossed back over one shoulder.

"Come sit down," Matt suddenly commanded, grasping her elbow to steer her to the edge of the creek bank. After she sank down onto the matted grass, he towered above her for so long she finally had no choice except to look up questioningly at him. At last he spoke. "The silent treatment becomes boring after a while, Charlotte."

"I'm not giving you the silent treatment," she said tersely. "I just didn't have anything to say. But if you want to talk, we'll talk. So, when's Didi getting back from Denver, tomorrow night or Monday morning?"

"Neither, probably. If I know Didi—and I think I do—she's had enough of the bucolic life. She may not come back."

"Not come back?" Charlotte repeated. "But how—I mean, she works for you. She's your assistant."

"And one of her employers is her father." Matt shrugged. "I'm sure she'll spend most of this weekend telling him how boring it is up here and begging him to let her work in our Denver office. In the end, he'll give in. That's the advantage of being the boss's daughter."

Charlotte wrinkled her nose. "They do seem to have a lot of advantages, don't they? Bosses' daughters, I mean."

"You sound as if you've had personal experience with some of them," Matt said perceptively as he lowered himself beside her. "Have you?"

"Haven't we all?" she hedged, unwilling to tell him what had happened with Brad. Resting back on her elbows, she hastily sidestepped her personal feelings. "What will you do if she doesn't come back? She al-

76

ways seemed to be running errands, so you must need an assistant."

"Not really. As I told you, I manufactured this job for her as a favor for her father. Since she was here, I thought she might as well get some idea of what a job is like, so I kept her busy. But if she's not here, the crew can handle any errands. They always have. But enough of this contrived conversation about Didi," Matt muttered, impatience tightening his features. He glared at her. "What I want to know is when you're going to stop treating me like I'm the enemy because I'm involved in this airport project. For God's sake, Charlotte, I'm only doing a job."

"I know that, but I can't forget that *your* decision might ruin Aunt Lou's life! If I could only make you understand, make you feel something—"

"Oh, you always make me feel something," he interrupted, his voice deceptively calm as his narrowed eyes raked over her. His hands closed around her upper arms and sat her up straight. "And right now, I'm tempted . . ."

"Tempted to what? Turn me over your knee?" Charlotte taunted foolishly. "Is that what you'd like to do?"

"Hardly. I don't think I'd get any thrill out of turning you over my knee. There are much more pleasurable ways to deal with you."

"Promises, promises," she shot back, then gasped as she was immediately eased back against the ground. Her eyes widened as Matt moved above her, but before she could utter her protest, his parted lips came down to cover her own, with a ravishing insistence. She struggled beneath him, but her efforts to escape were absolutely futile. His weight and strength thwarted all resistance, and when he caught both her wrists in one large hand and drew her arms back beside her head, she knew she was defeated. She went limp, hoping that unresponsiveness would succeed where struggle had failed. But as her tactics changed, his altered too. His weight shifted slightly, became more an evocative pressure as one leg confined both hers. His mouth, though still firm and masterful, began playing with hers. Charlotte tried to steel herself against the tantalizing effects of his kiss, determined not to respond, but she sensed in him a limitless patience that frightened her. The harder she concentrated on anything other than his touch, the more seductive that touch became. Drawing her arms around his shoulders, he released her hands, thus freeing his own, and that hand joined the other in exploring every graceful curve of her slender form.

A tremor fluttered across Charlotte's abdomen as Matt's hand molded her right hipbone then slipped around and down, following the shape of her buttocks. Gentle fingers pressed against her flesh and moved her closer to the hardening strength of his thighs.

Charlotte was swiftly losing the battle with her senses. A whirlpool of rippling sensations radiated through her, and when Matt nibbled the tender curve of her lower lip, the whirlpool became a tidal wave of delight. A rushing thrill shook her to the very core of her being, and her mouth was like an opening flower. A low triumphant groan rose from Matt as his lips plundered hers, taking with a hungry urgency that brooked no denial.

As if she could have denied him . . . Her fingers

tangled in the soft hair that grazed his nape and pressed downward, urging an even rougher possession of her mouth. She kissed him back, eagerly clinging to him, and her soft moan conveyed her delight as the tip of his tongue slipped inside her mouth. By then, kisses were no longer enough for either of them. She needed his touch all over, and he made no attempt to hide his need to touch. Turning onto his side, he covered her hipbone with one hand, holding her fast, vulnerable to the caresses he bestowed. Leaning on one arm over her, he trailed his other hand up the length of her, sweeping over shapely thighs and upward. The hard edge of his hand feathered her secret warmth, and when Charlotte gasped softly, he gripped her waist and pulled her into his arms. Her legs entangled with his.

"You're trembling," he whispered indulgently, his warm breath tickling her ear as he nibbled the lobe. Long fingers slipped through the golden cloud of her hair. "Tell me what you want, love."

"Kiss me."

When he did, sparks of fire leapt into flames, and the inner emptiness he had brought to life was aching to be filled; for the first time, Charlotte truly understood what it meant to need a man. Not any man, though—only this man. For her, only Matt could assuage the desires he had aroused. She was far beyond the ability to resist when he pulled off her sweater, then unfastened her sheer white bra. Her breath caught as he slowly peeled the lacy cups away from her sensitized skin. Her thickly lashed lids fluttered open and she found him gazing down at the rapid rise and fall of her breasts, his eyes a deep glowing amber.

His hands drifted up from her bare waist to cup her firm breasts. And when he lowered his head, he didn't relent. His lips sought and found one rosy peak, the moist pulling pressure rushing like fever over her, enlivening every nerve ending.

"Charlotte, I want you. So much I could make love to you right here, right now," he said huskily. Hard lips descended on hers with irresistible demand before he could see the hot color that swept up her throat to bloom in her cheeks. He did, however, feel her tremble beneath him. Lifting his head, he smiled lazily. "But this is hardly the place, is it? You're shivering." He glanced toward the house. "I know where the spare key to the house is. We can go there."

Part of her longed to agree, and she actually hesitated before finally shaking her head. Dropping her eyes, she said unevenly, "I . . . no, Matt, I can't. All this is happening much too fast."

"You're fighting the inevitable. We're going to have something very special together. You know it as well as I do," he said, the roughness in his voice seductive and enticing. "But if you need more time . . . Right now I think it would be wise for me to take you home. Put your clothes on, Charlotte."

She did, with haste and much fumbling, and she was grateful that after he had sat up and pulled her up beside him, he had looked away, as if he knew she was suffering a sudden overwhelming shyness. If he was that sensitive to her feelings . . . But no, she had decided he wasn't really a very sensitive man. Yet sometimes he seemed to be. He always treated Aunt Lou with kindness and respect. And whenever Charlotte was in his arms, she imagined he possessed the capacity for caring, but she was afraid that was sheer wishful thinking on her part, induced by the overpowering physical attraction between them.

Confused, she said nothing as she got to her feet, but as he rose and towered over her, she made herself look up at him. His slow, easy smile further accelerated pulses that were already too rapid. Her response to him seemed to be quite beyond her control. So, mostly to prove to herself that she still maintained some control, she drew back with a murmured protest when his hands spanned her waist and he started to kiss her again.

Her resistance didn't deter him. He laughed softly and shook his head indulgently. "Enchantress. You're determined to fight this, aren't you?" Running his lean fingers through her hair, he tilted her head back and lowered his until his lips hovered just above her own. "Give in, Charlotte," he whispered. "You might as well give in."

"Never. I'm not going to take Didi's place in your bed," she retorted, expecting a kiss in retaliation and feeling unreasonably disappointed when he released her. She looked up at his dark face, thought she detected a glimmer of amusement in his eyes, and felt even more bewildered. He had become a mystery again, one she longed to understand yet was afraid to explore, knowing she could get badly hurt in the process. An involvement with him would surely come to mean far too much to her while remaining only a casual affair to him. She couldn't allow that to happen, and to prevent it she knew she had to build up something akin to indifference to him. Well, she might as well start now, she thought.

With a slight smile she moved her hand in a dismissive gesture. "You've gotten the wrong idea about what I'm willing to give. If I gave you the wrong impression, then I'm sorry. But after all," she added, stretching up on tiptoe to press her lips lightly against his, "a kiss is just a kiss. It doesn't have to mean anything serious."

"You're playing with fire, Charlotte. I'm not a teenage boy you can tease or satisfy with kisses," he muttered, impatience replacing amusement in his eyes.

He pulled her so close against him that the tips of her toes barely grazed the ground, his arms were hard and unyielding around her. Yet his warm lips were evocatively gentle as they brushed slowly back and forth across hers until he achieved the response he sought. As she swayed against him, his mouth possessed hers with an intensity that made her dizzy. He kissed her again and again until her senses were aroused to a fever pitch. When he held her away from him at last, her breathing was as ragged as his. She gazed up at him, watching while he raked curiously unsteady fingers through his thick hair, his piercing eyes holding hers. There was no need for him to speak. He had proven quite effectively that his kisses were serious, mere preludes to an intimacy she didn't dare consider sharing with him; he was undoubtedly as ruthless in his personal relationships as he was in business.

How had she allowed herself to become so involved with him so quickly? she wondered. And more important, how was she going to escape the involvement unscathed? She couldn't run away. Her aunt needed her, Charlotte thought, and so she had to stay. She

was trapped with a man she found increasingly irresistible, despite all the misgivings she had about him.
What had happened to the common sense she had always possessed? With arousing kisses and caresses,
Matt was somehow able to drive all logical thought
out of her mind. And worst of all, he knew he could.

CHAPTER FIVE

On Tuesday Charlotte drove to Royal View to mail two designs to one of her clients. Though she had much to do back at the lodge, she cheerfully listened to all the news Mrs. Taggart wanted passed along to Aunt Lou, and was only required to nod now and then as the postmistress chattered on. When another patron entered the post office, drawing Mrs. Taggart's attention, Charlotte took the opportunity to wave good-bye and hastily make her getaway. After picking up a few items for herself and her aunt in the general store, she went to the service station, where the honorable mayor himself filled her nearly empty tank with gas. He had gossip to relate too, so she was delayed another ten minutes, but she really didn't mind. After life in a city, where so few people knew each other, it was comforting to live in a community where everyone knew everybody else's name. People cared about each other. Charlotte still believed that, although she couldn't help being disappointed that people had not rallied around Aunt Lou. Deep inside, she understood that the economically depressed county could benefit from an airport and development, and it was this understanding that kept her from feeling too bitter. If only Aunt Lou weren't caught in the middle, dangling, so to speak, while she waited to see if her beloved plateau would escape the bulldozers.

When the mayor's pleasant monologue wound to a close, Charlotte paid for the gas and headed for the lodge. Autumn's gentle winds sent an increasing number of leaves floating to the ground now, and there was a delicate aroma of hickory smoke drifting in the cool air. Opening her window a crack, Charlotte inhaled deeply, then frowned as she heard the wail of a siren in the distance, a sound that never failed to arouse a need in her to make certain those she cared about were safe. Almost of its own volition her foot pressed harder on the accelerator. When she turned onto the lane to the lodge, apprehension began to drag at the pit of her stomach. Though it was completely unfounded, she couldn't shake her increasing dread, and coming within sight of the lodge, she breathed a sigh of relief. Though Matt had been out when she'd left, his Jeep was now back, and to her surprise, knowing he was with Aunt Lou comforted her.

Her apprehension wasn't completely dissipated, however. She wasted no time parking the car and getting out, leaving her packages behind as she hurried toward the front steps. When the door suddenly swung open and Matt stepped out, she halted abruptly. One look at him and she knew something was wrong. Her face paled. "Oh, God! She's not . . . dead, is she?"

"No! No, she isn't," Matt assured her, taking the steps two at a time so he could enfold her in strong, supportive arms. Gentle hands stroked over her back, stilling her trembling. "She was having difficulty breathing, and though she insisted she'd be fine, I called an ambulance. She's being taken to the hospital in Juniper, about twenty miles from here. You know where it is?"

Nodding, Charlotte stood still, allowing Matt to dry away the tears which suddenly sprang to her eyes. "Was she conscious?" she finally asked, accepting the handkerchief he pressed into her hand. "Was it a heart attack?"

"She never lost consciousness, and she said she wasn't in pain. She seemed more frightened than anything else, because she couldn't catch her breath." Matt sighed. "My guess is that it wasn't actually a heart seizure, but I'm no doctor."

"Well, if it was a heart attack, I'm not surprised. That damned airport!" There was more defensive fear than resentment in her eyes as they flashed up at him. "I told you about her heart condition, and everybody in the county knows about it. All of you should have expected something like this to happen."

"Maybe trying to place blame will make you feel less helpless," Matt said without anger, reaching out with incredible gentleness to brush a hand over her hair. "Is that it? Does blaming me help you feel any better?"

"Oh, hell, no," she admitted thickly, too over-wrought to resist when he pulled her close again. Resting her forehead in the hollow of his shoulder, she groaned softly. "These days, nothing seems to make anything better. But I'll survive. It's Aunt Lou I'm concerned about. I have to get to her." Forcing a brave but tremulous smile to her lips, she moved away

86

from him. "Thank you for calling the ambulance. If you hadn't been here . . ."

"But I was. Come on. I'll drive you to the hospital."

"You don't have to do that."

"Of course I don't have to. I want to," he stated firmly. "For once, Charlotte, I'm not going to allow you to be so damned stubborn. Now, go get a toothbrush and whatever else Lou needs, and we'll leave."

Independent as she was, she had to admit she was relieved that he'd taken charge. His strength combined with her own and made it easier to cope with a situation that would have been far more difficult to face alone. Out of the lodge with her aunt's belongings and into the BMW in less than two minutes, she touched a hand to his muscular thigh after he had turned the car around.

"Thank you for taking me," she said sincerely. "It's very nice of you."

"Maybe I'm not quite the ogre you imagined," was his blunt reply. But he reassuringly clasped her hand in his, and didn't let go of it.

It was the longest twenty miles Charlotte had ever ridden. When she finally spotted the tiny white frame hospital on the outskirts of Juniper, she could hardly wait for Matt to stop the car so she could get out. He parked quickly and they entered a small reception area, but to Charlotte's dismay, the front desk was unattended. She looked around worriedly.

"This is such a little place," she whispered. "What if they can't give Aunt Lou the proper care here? Maybe I should have her transferred to a hospital in Denver."

"We'll cross that bridge when we come to it. We

don't even know how ill Lou is yet. Besides, I've heard good things about this hospital. The facilities may not be the most modern, but the doctor in charge is competent and well respected." Guiding her to a small sofa, he made her sit down. "Someone will be out in a moment who can tell us something, I'm sure."

A nurse-receptionist did appear not thirty seconds later, but all she could tell Charlotte and Matt was that Louisa was in an examining room and a doctor was with her. Finally, after Charlotte had fidgeted away the next ten minutes, the doctor himself appeared, striding down a long hallway, his white coat flapping around his knees. A tall, loose-limbed angular man with thinning brown hair, he came over to the sofa.

"You're Lou's niece?"

"Yes, Charlotte Jordan," she replied. When the doctor's gaze shifted to Matt, who had remained standing, she added, "And this is Matt Royall, a guest at Aunt Lou's lodge. How is she?"

"Resting now," the doctor said, removing his stethoscope and folding it into his pocket. "She's been given a sedative, which is just what she needed. She told me she's been upset about this airport project your county's proposing, and it's obvious to me she's worried about it to the point of nervous exhaustion."

Sitting on the edge of a sofa cushion, Charlotte looked up at him. "Then she didn't have a heart attack, Doctor . . . uh . . ."

"Sommers," he provided brusquely. "No, it wasn't a heart attack this time. But if she goes on fretting like she has been, she's going to have one soon. Her heart's not in the best condition, but I'm sure you know that."

"Yes. But even so, I don't really see how we're going to stop her from fretting about the airport." Charlotte gestured helplessly. "How can she stop worrying about it?"

"She's going to have to try. People kill themselves all the time by worrying about things they can't possibly change. Lou's simply going to have to accept the fact that the airport's going to be built near her lodge."

"But we don't know that for sure yet," Charlotte protested. "Other sites are still being considered."

"Not very seriously, from what I hear."

"What does that mean?" A shadow of suspicion settled over Charlotte's face as she looked quickly at Matt, then back to the doctor. "What have you heard, Dr. Sommers?"

"Seems to be a foregone conclusion that the airport will be located on the plateau behind Lou's lodge," the doctor replied, scowling. "Pity. Lou's a fine woman. I hate to see this happening to her at her age."

"That may be a foregone conclusion on the grapevine, Dr. Sommers," Matt intervened, "but Charlotte's right. No decision's been made yet concerning the site. I'm the engineer in charge of the project, and we're still in the process of surveying all the potential locations."

"I see." The doctor nodded thoughtfully. "Well, seems like some of the facts got lost while that story was being passed along. But no matter what, Lou must accept the fact that the airport might be built on her land." He turned to Charlotte again. "You'll have to help her do that. Try to make her understand that the

89

situation's beyond her control, and that no amount of hoping or worrying is going to help."

"That's easier said than done," Charlotte murmured. "But I'll do what I can."

"I'll talk to her about it too, before I let her go home. That'll probably be early next week," Dr. Sommers said. Deciding to be sociable then, he extended a hand to the younger man. "Matt, pleased to meet you. I recognized your name. How's the project going so far?"

"Right on schedule. We're collecting data and doing the surveying now, so we'll be ready to start the actual construction as soon as possible next spring."

"May I see Aunt Lou now?" Charlotte spoke up tersely, in no mood to listen to talk about the airport. Having gained both men's attention, she stood and added politely, "Please."

"Tomorrow would be better," Dr. Sommers declared. "What she needs right now is complete quiet and a long uninterrupted sleep."

"But if she wakes up and I'm not here . . ."

"I'm sure she'll realize you haven't deserted her," Matt said with a gentle smile of understanding. He shook the doctor's hand again. "We'll go now, but I'm sure Charlotte will be back on the doorstep as early as possible in the morning."

Nodding, Charlotte gave Dr. Sommers a grateful smile before Matt led her toward the door. Outside, the late afternoon sun was casting an orange glow on a few scattered clouds and the snowcapped peaks, and by the time they had driven back to Royal View, dusk was falling. Deciding she shouldn't have to prepare a meal, Matt insisted they eat out. He took her to the only place in town, the tiny café beside the post office, where the items on the menu were few but sufficient. Both of them chose Western steaks, unsurprisingly the specialty of the house, and it looked so delicious that Charlotte regained her appetite.

Stars were studding a black velvet sky when Matt and Charlotte returned to the lodge, and the moment she stepped inside ahead of him, she realized with a sudden lurch of her heart that the two of them would be completely alone; Didi had remained in Denver, as Matt had supposed she would, and there were no other guests at the lodge.

Charlotte gladly accepted the glass of white wine Matt poured for her and poised herself on one arm of the sofa while he mixed a drink for himself. Absently twirling a strand of hair around one finger, she smiled at him when he joined her. Reaching out from where he stood, he stilled her hand, then disentangled her hair.

"Charlotte, Lou's getting the best care tonight," he assured her, without releasing her hand. "Try not to worry."

"I'm trying. I know you're right," she murmured, her fingertips grazing his palm as she stood. "I should probably get busy to take my mind off everything. I have a lot of work to do anyway." She walked to the rolltop desk. "I'd planned to start the site drawing of the plateau tonight. But I might need your help."

"Just yell if you do," he said agreeably. "I'll be right here."

Far too aware of that fact during the following two hours, Charlotte's nervousness increased every time she had to ask Matt a question, and she was forced to ask several. When Matt came over to answer them, he invariably leaned over the desk, one arm on the back of her chair, and as often as not, his long fingers brushed against her back. Sometimes his touch seemed to deliberately linger, and she would be overcome by the ridiculous notion that he might actually be able to hear her heart thudding. Only when he went to sit back down on the sofa did her breathing return to normal. Finally she tried to solve a problem, and after staring at the drawing for nearly ten minutes, conceded defeat and called Matt over.

"You've worked long enough tonight," he announced softly, interrupting her question and brushing aside her hand as she massaged the back of her neck, replacing it with his own strong fingers. Gently kneading the tensed muscles, he evoked a sigh of pleasure from her. When Charlotte tilted her head to one side, silently encouraging him to continue, he swept her up in his arms to carry her to the sofa.

"Turn over," he ordered softly. When she hesitated, he bent down to ease her to her stomach, ignoring her halfhearted protest. He sat down on the sofa beside her, and without warning, pushed her sweater far up her back.

Charlotte almost gasped as he swiftly unfastened her bra. She tried to rise, then felt as if a burning heat had suffused every inch of her skin when his hand relentlessly pressed her down again. "I don't really need a back massage," she murmured, her voice strained. "You don't have to do this."

Matt did it anyway. Without answering her, he pulled her arms down to her sides, forcing her into a more relaxed position. His large competent hands descended to her shoulders and rubbed circles down over her back. His thumbs probed the delicate structure of her spine while his fingers coaxed the tension from the muscles across her back and around to her sides. Charlotte submitted to a touch so enjoyable that she felt she might melt into the cushions. As the strain of the day seeped away, she closed her eyes and breathed a long contented sigh.

"Mmm, now that you've started, I might not let you stop," she murmured dreamily. "That really feels so good."

"Does this feel good too?" he questioned huskily, brushing firm parted lips across the center of her back. A tremor of pleasure rippled through her, and his hands spanned her bare waist while he scattered light, enticing kisses from smooth creamy shoulders downward to the small of her back. "And this? Do you like this?"

"Yes."

She did like it, far too much to resist when he turned her over and his lips sought her exposed midriff. Her hands cupped his face, her fingertips tracing the contours of his ears as she urged his mouth up to her own, delighting in the weight of his body pressing her down into the sofa. Matt kissed her with languid insistence, catching the fullness of her lower lip between his before trailing the tip of his tongue along the upper curve. Wrapping her arms around his neck, she molded herself to him, moving with him when he turned onto his side. His hand followed the graceful lines of her waist and hip, down to where her corduroy skirt was twisted up around her thighs. The searing passion she had always sensed just beneath his surface was suddenly unleashed, and the swift hardening of his lips was echoed throughout the length of his body.

His obvious desire heightened her own. When he took off her sweater and removed her bra with it, and his hands began playing over her straining breasts and she delighted in his caressing possession. Yet the need for complete fulfillment was rising in her, and as she realized how very close she was to total surrender, she dragged herself back from the world of erotic pleasure where he had taken her. Exercising every ounce of control she could muster, she shook her head and escaped his embrace. "No, Matt," she said firmly. "I'm not going to let you take advantage of the fact that I'm upset about Aunt Lou. Just because I'm more vulnerable now—"

"God, spare me more of your ridiculous accusations," he muttered disgustedly. Sitting up, he raked his hand through his hair. "If this is your way of punishing me for what's happening to Lou, I'm warning you, Charlotte, that you'd be foolish to start something like this again without being prepared for a very different reaction from me. I won't let you say no again."

"Are you threatening to force—"

"I'm threatening to teach you a lesson about men you obviously haven't learned yet." His gaze narrowed and roamed searchingly over her face. "In every other way you're a sensible woman, so I don't believe you're naturally a tease. Maybe you're so caught up in your aunt's problems and so determined to believe I'm the enemy that you feel guilty about responding to me the way you do. So you pull away."

"If I wanted to be analyzed, I'd go to a psychiatrist.

Right now all I want to do is go to bed. Good night," she said stiffly. She stood, walked across the room and up the stairs, grateful that he hadn't guessed the true reason she wouldn't, *couldn't,* let their relationship evolve into intimacy. Guilt no longer had anything to do with her need to resist him. In fact it was becoming increasingly difficult to think of him as the enemy. When he treated her as he had earlier tonight, with tenderness and compassion, she realized how very easy it would be to fall in love with him. Though she was so attracted to him that she never seemed able to resist his kisses, a strong instinct for self-preservation always overcame her desire to surrender. She didn't want to be hurt. In her heart she knew that an intimate involvement with Matt would undoubtedly leave her with deep emotional scars when everything between them ended.

Early Saturday morning Charlotte padded back upstairs after answering the phone in her aunt's diminutive office adjoining the kitchen. As she walked down the hall, she paused outside Matt's room. She tilted her head to one side and thought she heard sounds of activity inside. After hesitating for another moment, she shrugged and knocked lightly on the door, opening it when she was told to come in.

"I'm in here shaving," Matt called from the bathroom. "What is it, Charlotte?"

"Thought you might like to know you can go back to bed if you want to. We're up at the crack of dawn for nothing," she answered, stopping short when she reached the open doorway and found Matt standing before the mirror, naked except for the towel he'd hitched low around his hips after his shower. Fascinated by long powerful legs, taut stomach, and the breadth of his shoulders and chest, she was unable to look away until he turned to her with a questioning look. Riveting her gaze on his brown neck, she explained, "I just took a phone call from the man we were expecting to arrive today. When I told him Aunt Lou was ill and wouldn't be here, he said he was sure his wife would want to postpone their trip."

"Good. You have enough to do without dealing with guests," he pronounced, giving his hair a quick brushing without even glancing back at the mirror. His ablutions completed, he leaned on one hand in the doorway. "Now that they're not coming, maybe you can relax."

"Maybe," she agreed, but she doubted it. She had never felt less relaxed than she did at this moment, with him clad in a provocative towel and she in a skimpy gown covered by a robe that suddenly didn't seem nearly thick enough. Barely able to stand still under his wandering gaze as it drifted slowly over her, she clenched her hands into fists in her pockets but tried not to let her uneasiness show on her face.

As the silence between them lengthened, she felt compelled to break it. "Well, that's all I had to tell you. I'll let you get dressed now. Or are you going back to bed?"

He shook his head. "Are you?"

"No. I had a cup of coffee while I was downstairs, so I'd probably never get back to sleep."

"I have an idea then," he said, straightening to move closer to her. "You've been tense since Lou went into the hospital, but there's something we could do today to make you relax."

"What . . . do you mean?"

As Charlotte glanced involuntarily at the wide bed, Matt smiled wryly and shook his head, playfully tugging a silken tendril of her hair. "That's not what I had in mind, Charlotte, but if you'd prefer a day in bed with me to a picnic, I certainly won't object."

"A picnic will suffice," she retorted pertly, unable to suppress a smile when he laughed.

It was a warm enough day for a picnic, especially on the sun-drenched meadow Matt and Charlotte had found a half mile east of Royal View. After a leisurely walk in an adjoining wood, they ate the lunch she had packed in a wicker basket. It was a companionable time, filled with conversation both serious and light. Charlotte discovered Matt had a delightful sense of humor, which was enhanced by his ability to laugh at himself. And as she had noticed on several other occasions, he was a versatile man, interested in too many subjects to ever be boring.

Relaxing and enjoyable as the afternoon was, it sped by too fast for her. When Charlotte remembered to glance at her wristwatch, she was dismayed to see it was already after three. When she explained it was nearly time for her daily visit to Louisa, Matt surprised her by saying he would go with her to see her aunt. He surprised her again later by driving past the hospital and on to the small town of Juniper, where he stopped at a shop and bought a lovely white lawn nightgown that looked as if it had been tailor-made for Louisa.

Louisa was thrilled. When she opened the gift there

was a sparkle of excitement in her eyes that Charlotte hadn't seen for a very long time. Holding the gown up against herself, Louisa actually smiled coquettishly at Matt.

"This is so pretty. Thank you," she said. "It's been years since I got something so beautiful from such a handsome young man."

Matt's response was as flirtatious, and as he earned Louisa's full attention for the next several minutes, her inner youth once again appeared glowingly on her face. Sitting by the bed, Charlotte watched her aunt and Matt, and gratitude for what he was doing swelled up in her. He was genuinely fond of her aunt. Charlotte was looking up at him so intently that it took her a second or two to realize that Louisa was trying to hand her the crewel embroidery piece she was working on while in the hospital.

"As long as you're just sitting there doing nothing, would you make French knots to fill the center of that blue flower for me?" Aunt Lou requested, giving her the hoop with cream cloth stretched taut across it. She grinned up at Matt. "I taught her how to embroider, except for French knots. I never could do a good one. Charlotte learned from her mother and tried to teach me, but you know what they say about old dogs and new tricks. Now I just make her do them for me."

Smiling to herself, Charlotte deftly threaded a needle with fine gold yarn and began to make the tiny French knots, starting in the flower's center. Becoming engrossed in work she enjoyed, she didn't bother to brush back her hair when it fell forward on both sides to graze against her cheeks. It was like a golden frame around her face when she sensed Matt watching her and looked up. Something indefinable but exciting in his tawny eyes captured and held her bemused gaze. When a secret smile touched his lips and he inclined his head toward Louisa, who was still stroking the fine fabric of her gown, a rushing warmth spread in Charlotte's chest until she felt as if she would be consumed by it. She finally admitted to herself that all her confusing feelings toward Matt had merged into only one —a growing love.

CHAPTER SIX

Charlotte did as Dr. Sommers had advised. Louisa had been out of the hospital a week, and whenever she mentioned the airport, Charlotte subtly tried to help her accept the possibility that the plateau might be chosen as the site. She knew it was only wise to do so. False hopes raised too high now could very well be shattered later, and Charlotte wasn't sure her aunt's heart was strong enough to bear an unexpected disappointment of that magnitude. It was better to prepare her for the worst.

Still, Charlotte continued to hope for the best. On a cold and overcast Thursday she drove out to take a second look at the meadow beside the gray stone house, before beginning the elevation drawing of it. As she gazed out over the flat grassy expanse, she still thought it looked like a perfect location for an airfield. Leaning back against the front fender of her car, she made a quick sketch of the meadow to serve as a memory refresher later, and with every stroke of her pencil, she was hoping Matt would discover that the flooding here wasn't too severe. She had to hope that because she had visited the other sites, and none was as suitable as the plateau.

With a soft sigh Charlotte finished the line sketch and slipped her pencil into her hair above her ear. Though she hoped against hope that the airport would be located here, she still thought it would be a shame to destroy the tiny valley's tranquility with the roar of plane engines. She lifted her shoulders in a resigned shrug. There was always a price to be paid for progress, she supposed. Lost in her reverie, Charlotte leaned against the Omni for a long time, simply looking at the lovely hills that tumbled down to the meadow. When the tip of her nose began to tingle from exposure to the cold wind, she realized how long she had been standing there.

Snow started to fall when Charlotte got into her car and switched on the motor. By the time she pulled out onto the main road, she had to use the windshield wipers to sweep away the flakes. Snow in October was not uncommon in the Rockies, but this one threatened to become a major storm, according to the weather report Charlotte had heard earlier on the radio. Remembering the ominous forecast, she increased her speed and almost immediately regretted it when a jackrabbit hopped across the road in front of her. With a startled gasp she automatically swerved toward the far side of the highway, tried to straighten the car too quickly, and fishtailed the rear left wheel into a side ditch. After the jolting stop, she uttered an explicit curse. In all the years she'd been driving, she had never had even a minor accident. She had to have her first one now, she thought with dismay, on an infrequently traveled road in a raging snowstorm. Well, it wasn't exactly a *raging* storm, she conceded, but she still would prefer being back at the lodge to being

101

stuck out here. Though she felt sure it was useless, she gunned the engine, hoping to escape the ditch, and was hardly surprised when she didn't move an inch. Switching on the blinking emergency lights, she folded her arms across her chest and began the wait for a passing motorist who would be kind enough to stop and help.

A long half hour passed. Knowing she might have to wait a very long time for someone to come, she decided her only other alternative was to walk back to the gray stone house. Matt had mentioned a spare key, and although Charlotte didn't relish the idea of letting herself into a stranger's home, she knew that people in the Rockies understood that people stranded by weather sometimes had to resort to drastic measures or pay dearly for their mistakes. She didn't think the owners of the house would mind if she took temporary shelter there. Saying a silent prayer that they hadn't disconnected their phone for the winter, Charlotte pulled her wool hat down over her ears. She removed her key from the ignition and got out of the car, but left the emergency lights blinking.

Gray skies hastened the twilight, and it was nearly dark when Charlotte reached the house. Stepping into the recessed doorwell for a moment to escape the biting wind, she rubbed cheeks that were stinging from the peppering of icy snow. Then, wasting no more time for fear of losing what little daylight remained, she began searching for the house key.

It wasn't under the mat, nor on top of one of the two brass and glass lanterns by the doorway. She sighed wearily. Obviously one member of this household was tall, because there was really only one logical place left where the key might be. Reaching it was the problem. Luckily, the lawn was scattered with fallen twigs from the trees. She found a long stout one and went back to sweep one end of it over the top of the door frame. To her immense relief, a key clattered down onto the flagstone at her feet.

Charlotte hastily unlocked the door and stepped inside to a carpeted foyer. She fumbled for the light switch and was delighted when all the small lights of a crystal chandelier flared above her. Only minimally aware of the lovely decor, she set out to find a telephone, coming upon it in the study across the foyer from the living room. When she lifted the receiver, the dial tone was like music to her ears. She hurriedly called the service station in Royal View, but no one was there, so she dialed the mayor's home number. His wife answered and Charlotte explained her situation.

"Lawd, honey, Gilbert's had to take the wrecker up to Carson pass. Four or five car pileup up there. And the snow's already so deep in Carson that I don't expect Gilbert back any time soon. Maybe you should call the highway patrol."

"Oh, no, I'm sure they have their hands full with more serious accidents than mine," Charlotte said, then added reluctantly, "Anyway, a guest at Aunt Lou's lodge can probably come out here to get me. I'll call him."

After expressing her thanks and saying good-bye, Charlotte broke the connection. She hesitated a moment, not particularly eager to ask Matt to rescue her, but decided she had no other choice and dialed her aunt's number. After convincing Louisa that she hadn't been injured, Charlotte was told that Matt hadn't returned to the lodge yet. Her aunt then reassured her that he would come for her the moment he got back. Wishing he were already on the way, Charlotte sighed inwardly, but told Louisa not to worry about her and hung up.

For the first time she noticed the chill in the house. Though she could hear the distant whir of the furnace, the thermostat had obviously been set only high enough to prevent the pipes from freezing. Whatever the temperature in the house was, it wasn't warm enough for human comfort. She pushed her coat collar up to her neck again as she walked across the foyer into the living room. It was lovely, decorated in muted blues and reds, with a white area rug covering part of the gleaming hardwood floor. But it seemed too spacious and lonely. Charlotte went back to the study and curled up in a winged leather chair in front of a cold fireplace. A sense of isolation was sweeping over her, accentuated by the wind whistling lonesomely in the eaves.

The rumble of an approaching Jeep about ninety minutes later was the most beautiful sound Charlotte had ever heard. She jumped from the chair and practically flew to the front door, but didn't open it until she heard the Jeep door slam. The air was so thick with falling snow, that Matt was only about fifteen feet from the house when Charlotte finally saw him. She rushed out and flung herself into his arms.

"Oh, thank God you came," she exclaimed, her voice muffled against his neck. "I was so afraid I might have to spend the night here and—"

"You afraid, Charlotte? I didn't think that was possible," he murmured, an arm around her waist holding her close against him as he walked back into the house and closed the door behind them. Turning her to him, he draped his hands over her shoulders and looked somberly down at her. "What's wrong? You're trembling. Has something scared you?"

She gave him an almost sheepish smile. "I guess I scared myself. I felt so odd being in a strange house, and then . . . oh, it's silly."

"Tell me anyway."

"Well, it was so quiet and isolated, and the wind sounds so creepy when it whips through the pines. . . ."

"What an imagination you have," Matt admonished, fighting a chuckle and losing the battle. When his deep, muted laughter evoked an answering smile, he drew her into his arms again, one hand stroking her hair. "But now you feel safer?"

She nodded. "Much safer. Thank you for coming. I know it was a lot of trouble but—"

"Never mind that," he cut in, looking over her head into the study. "Why didn't you start a fire in the fireplace? There's plenty of wood right there beside it. No wonder your cheeks are like ice. It's cold in here."

Charlotte followed when he released her and strode into the study. "Well, I didn't think I should start a fire because it might not be easy to put out when you came to get me."

"You shouldn't have worried about that," Matt told her, looking back at her as he snapped a small piece of kindling over his knee and tossed the sticks onto the grate. "We won't need to put the fire out because we can't possibly drive back to the lodge tonight."

"Are the roads that bad already?"

"Up toward the lodge they're worse than here. I'm not going to risk going back in the dark. We may be able to leave tomorrow if it stops snowing or slows, and the snowplows can clear the road.

Charlotte nodded. "I'll call Aunt Lou and tell her we can't get back tonight."

"I told her we wouldn't be able to before I left the lodge," Matt said, striking a long match to ignite the kindling. The fire blazed up, crackling and popping. He placed two small split logs on the flames, then straightened to look at Charlotte with a reassuring smile. "She sent some milk, eggs, and bread to go with what we have in the pantry and the freezer here. We won't have to subsist on canned soup while we're marooned."

"I'm not even sure there's a can of soup in the house. I haven't been in the kitchen."

"You must be hungry then. I am. You build up the fire while I get the provisions Lou sent from the Jeep. Then we can throw together a meal."

As it turned out, what Charlotte "threw together" was a delicious fluffy omelet and a salad made with the fixings Lou had sent. For dessert they had cheese and apples, also sent by Lou, but it was the steaming mugs of hot buttered rum that Matt prepared which really made Charlotte begin to feel warm again. After cleaning up the dishes, Matt directed her back into the study where they could relax with the drinks by the fire. Outside the wind still howled, but it no longer sounded so hauntingly lonely to Charlotte.

When Matt sat down in the chair she'd curled up in earlier, she sank down onto the soft rug at his feet, directly in front of the blazing fire. Basking in the warmth that allowed her to finally remove her coat, she tugged her light blue sweater down farther over her hips and looked back at him.

"I can't tell you how glad I am you're here," she said seriously, impulsively laying a hand on his knee. "If you hadn't come, I think I might have spent the entire night shivering and shaking and imagining I heard footsteps on the stairs. I don't know why. I'm not a very skittish person."

"No one likes to be alone in a storm," Matt said with quiet understanding, then watched her over the rim of his mug as he took a sip. "So I'm glad I was able to get here. By the way, I stopped by your car and turned off the emergency lights. They were getting pretty dim anyway; the battery wouldn't have lasted much longer."

"I doubt anyone would have driven past to see them blinking anyway. Since I've been here, I haven't heard anyone go by. Surely this isn't the only house in the valley?"

"There are two or three others, but there isn't another one for miles in the direction you were going. You're lucky you went into the ditch close enough to be able to walk back here."

"I know. It would have been awful if I'd had to spend the night in the car," Charlotte agreed. "I still feel strange about just unlocking the door and coming into this house. But you'd mentioned you know the owner, so that made me feel a little less like I was breaking and entering."

"The man who owns this house would rather you be here than in your car for the night," Matt murmured, leaning forward slightly in the chair, the expression on his dark face unreadable and mysterious. For an instant he seemed on the verge of saying something important, but at last he shook his head and merely added, "So stop worrying about being here. No one could possibly blame you for coming in out of a storm like this."

Knowing he was right, Charlotte nodded, then turned her attention back to the fire. As she took tiny sips of the hot drink, she slowly began to relax, and realized the events of the day had made her unusually tired. Soon her head began to feel too heavy, so she leaned it against Matt's knee, smiling lazily when he lightly stroked her hair. Wrapped in a cocoon of warmth and companionable silence, she was nearly asleep when a sudden thudding noise upstairs brought her to full awareness.

"What was that?" she whispered, jerking her head around to look at Matt. "Did you hear that sound?"

"It was only a log shifting. While you were making dinner, I started a fire in the fireplace in the bedroom just above the study," Matt explained, then smiled and shook his head indulgently when she breathed a heartfelt sigh of relief. "I'm here with you, Charlotte. You're not supposed to imagine that every noise you hear is the sound of footsteps on the stairs. You're not alone now. Of course, maybe you don't really trust me. I promise you I didn't even bring an ax with me in the Jeep."

"Oh, stop that," she chided, laughing at his joke and at herself. Then, as his smile abruptly faded, hers did too.

Something other than amusement now glinted in his

eyes, and she was unable to look away from him, unable to draw back when he leaned forward to easily lift her up onto his lap. The beige crewneck sweater that covered his light blue shirt was softly inviting beneath her fingertips, and of their own volition, her hands swept slowly back and forth across his chest. The light in his eyes flared, issuing an unmistakable warning that she no longer wanted to heed, and when powerful arms slipped around her, crushing her to him, she didn't protest. His mouth covered hers, parting her lips with searing urgency. He hadn't touched her in nearly two weeks, and the passion that had always erupted between them seemed like nothing compared to the desires they aroused in each other now. Charlotte clung to him as he stood with her in his arms and started out of the study to the stairs. Her heart gave one quick little jerk, then all remaining fear was swept away in a sweet tide of inevitability when he started up the steps. Her love surged forth and expanded to an irrepressible need to give everything of herself and to take everything from him.

Words were unnecessary as Matt carried Charlotte into a spacious bedroom decorated in earth colors. A man's room, she thought with only a modicum of interest, which vanished entirely when he lowered her to her feet beside a wide bed. Moving around her, he tossed more wood on the fire, giving her only a moment to catch her breath before he returned and smoothly removed her sweater and tweed slacks. Then he unclipped her bra and allowed it to drift with a whisper of sound to the floor, to be joined almost immediately by her panties. Under the approving gaze

109

that wandered over her, Charlotte stood very still, her heart pounding uncontrollably with anticipation.

At last she could await his touch no longer. Taking his hands in hers, she brought them around her waist, gasping softly as her initiative evoked an impassioned response. Matt pulled her to him, bending her back against supporting arms while he kissed her again and again, each kiss deepening until her legs were invaded by a delicious weakness. She trembled. He eased her gently down on the bed, bringing the covers up around her shoulders to keep her warm.

Closing her eyes, she tried to remind herself of the magnitude of what she was about to do, but love and passion had become inseparable, and together they easily overcame caution. Her eyes opened again, deep pools of emerald as she watched him quickly undress. Even when he switched out the bedside lamp, the room was bathed in the fire's amber glow and she could see him clearly. He leaned over her, his skin as dark as burnished copper against the fairness of hers when he brushed the covers down slightly to press his hand between her breasts.

"Your heart's pounding again, Charlotte," he murmured with a slight knowing smile. "But not exactly for the same reason it pounded the first time I kissed you, is it?"

"Not exactly," she whispered, smiling when he traced a finger across her lips and she caught the tip gently between her teeth.

He lowered himself to the bed beside her, and she reached out to him, her arms tightening eagerly around his shoulders as her soft mouth met his. The scent of his skin, the hardness of his lithe body, his

110

caressing touch and kisses, were soon all that existed for her. She returned his kisses with a consuming passion, her mouth opening to the tongue that sought the sweetness within. She became warm and pliant as Matt explored every enticing curve of her body with demanding yet tender hands. Her own hands moved with feverish wonder over his broad chest and shoulder, outlining the contours of corded muscles with her fingertips.

A weakening heat like she had never known before coursed through her veins, kindling fires that danced over every inch of her skin wherever he touched her. Feeling vibrantly alive as his caresses became more demanding, she surrendered with a sigh when he cupped her breasts in his hands, bringing them to throbbing fullness with his mouth. The tip of his tongue flicked over and around each nipple until it peaked, then he possessed them completely by closing his mouth around each swollen crest, making her senses swim.

He was making her crazy. She wanted him to stop; she wanted him to never stop; and she was powerless to prevent her legs from parting slightly, invitingly, when his hand slipped between her thighs. She moaned with the aching emptiness that expanded inside her as his thumb brushed upward to feather over her. Her eyes opened drowsily and she watched as he lowered his head to trail a burning strand of kisses across her abdomen.

She felt utterly lost in the passion of his gaze when he looked at her. Then he moved with swift urgency to claim her mouth again, his lips teasing hers lightly until she begged for more forceful kisses. When he at last complied, and plundered the sweetness of her mouth, the desire to belong to him had become sheer necessity. She moved instinctively against him, her slender young body tempting him, promising delights he had no will to refuse. With a soft groan muffled in the glorious thickness of her hair, he gripped her waist, turned her onto her back, and trailed a hand up along her thighs.

At his touch Charlotte tensed, but only for an instant before a maelstrom of devastating sensations caught her up in tumultuous excitement and her parted lips hungrily sought his.

His intimate exploration continued even as he whispered hoarsely against her mouth, "I didn't realize you'd never . . . Charlotte, love, I hope you know what you're doing, because I can't stop now."

"I don't want you to stop," she confessed breathlessly, a glowing light in her soft green eyes as his kisses and caresses gentled in consideration of her innocence. Trembling hands cupped his beloved face, then feathered down to cling to his shoulders as he moved above her.

There was an unspoken promise in his amber eyes as he looked down at her, a promise that he was capable of great tenderness despite the intensity of his need for her. "Try to relax," he coaxed, kissing her gently. "Don't be afraid of me, Charlotte. I'll try not to hurt you."

His hand slipped beneath her hips and he pulled her upward. Though he whispered her name coaxingly again, she couldn't relax completely. She expected pain, and when he entered her with a gentle thrust, pain came, piercing and keen for a fraction of a second, then fading to a memory forever overshadowed by the joy of love. Charlotte pressed her nails into the corded muscles of Matt's shoulders as narrowness yielded warmly to the invasion of powerful masculinity. Her first soft cry was lost in the shuddering sigh of pleasure that followed, and that sigh was muffled by his mouth capturing hers. With successive strokes he filled her completely, taking possession of her deepest emotions as well as her physical being.

The union of their bodies merely deepened her love for him, as she had known intimacy would, and all her intrinsic warmth and capacity to give surged forth to become her precious gift to him. His tender consideration and patience seemed boundless, making her love him all the more. Holding his own blazing desires under strict control, he slowly transported her to a world she had never truly believed existed. In the fire's golden glow, he taught her all the pleasures they could share as intimate delights were prolonged then repeated, bringing each of them closer and closer to fulfillment, until at last she was trembling with aching desires so intense she thought she would cry out if they weren't soon assuaged.

"Oh, Matt," she whispered breathlessly, her lips feverishly seeking his.

All inhibitions had vanished, and she wrapped herself around him, and learning that she could exercise some power over him too. Her response snapped his control, and passion erupted to engulf them both. She cried his name out softly while cascading waves of pleasure rippled within her, until she felt almost faint with delight. As the throbbing slowed, leaving in its wake an incredible sense of completion, she pressed her hands down hard on Matt's lean naked hips, eager to give satisfaction to him. No longer capable of gentleness, he growled her name and found his own fulfillment with such obvious pleasure that tears of joy filled her eyes.

After, they lay close together, legs still entangled, arms wrapped around each other while their breathing began to slow. Adrift in a magical sense of belonging, Charlotte lazily traced her fingertips along the smooth skin of his collarbone, then feathered them down to brush over the hard nubs of his flat brown nipples.

"Watch it, love," he warned, gazing at her through sleepy eyes. "Keep that up and we'll start all over again."

A soft smile curved her lips, but when he kissed the tip of her small nose, she allowed her eyes to drift shut. Contented, she nestled close against him and soon slipped into untroubled sleep.

Some time in the night a kiss awakened her. She slowly opened her eyes and found Matt slipping back into bed beside her and drawing the covers snugly over both of them.

"Just adding more wood to the fire," he explained, then smiled indulgently when she stretched lazily. Drawing her to him, he brushed a kiss over her tousled hair as he murmured, "I hope you aren't feeling any regrets, Charlotte. I suppose I should feel guilty about taking your virginity, but I'm not sorry at all. You're a delight."

"Despite my inexperience?"

"Despite even that," he teased, placing a light kiss on her temple.

Relieved that the dim light hid the blush that rose in

114

her cheeks, she snuggled closer to him, smiling when his arm tightened around her possessively. She basked in the warmth of his affection. For weeks she had tried to suppress the hope that Matt could fall in love with her, but now that hope bloomed so swiftly that she had no chance to nip it in the bud. She gathered it to her heart, needing to hold it there. Tonight she had committed herself to him without hesitation; now she had to believe he had made some sort of commitment too. She would simply have to be patient, she thought dreamily, seeking the hollow of his shoulder for a pillow as she released a slow tremulous breath.

"Tell me what you're thinking," Matt whispered close to her ear. "Is it about Brad?"

Charlotte's eyes flew open and she looked at him. "How do you know about Brad? Did Aunt Lou—"

"She mentioned him. She was concerned about you, since he'd decided to see someone else."

"He dropped me the moment he met the daughter of his boss, if you want to know the truth," Charlotte said with a rueful smile. "But Aunt Lou shouldn't worry about past history. And she shouldn't have mentioned Brad to you."

"How serious was your relationship with him?" Matt persisted, his tawny eyes searching her face. "What did he mean to you?"

"I'm not sure anymore. Maybe he was just a habit. I guess I thought something permanent might come of our relationship, but we really hadn't gotten very serious."

"I wondered if you might still care about Brad," he murmured, cupping her chin in one large hand as a smile touched his mouth. "Charlotte, love, you've become very important to me."

"Really?" she whispered back, happiness washing over her so swiftly that she could scarcely catch her breath. He hadn't said he loved her, but for the moment, she was content. Slipping her arms around his neck, she gazed up at him. "Are you absolutely sure you mean that?"

He nodded. "Absolutely sure."

"Oh Matt, I—" Before caution could stop her, she started to say she loved him, but the words were caught unspoken in the savage insistence of his kiss.

They made love again, this time with a surer knowledge of each other. As her initiation in lovemaking continued, both she and Matt discovered what an ardent young woman she could be. Passions she had always suppressed were now rising to equal the strength of his. Matt knew precisely how to sweep her away in a tide of irresistible delight. And when release came for both of them and they drifted down together from the heights of desires fulfilled, she lay wrapped in his arms, warm and relaxed and once again glad she had given love, even if she'd never said the words.

"Matt," she said softly several minutes later, touching her lips to the slowing pulse beat in his throat. "Do you think they'll get the road cleared tomorrow?"

"Probably. But why do you ask?" he answered, a hint of amusement in his resonant voice. "Afraid you'll have to spend another night here with me?"

She shook her head. "It isn't that. I guess I'm just a little worried about Aunt Lou being alone in the lodge."

"That bothered me too, so when I passed by the

116

hotel in Royal View last night on my way here, I sent one of the surveyors to the lodge to stay with her."

"That does make me feel better, but . . ."

"What else is bothering you?" he questioned when she hesitated. "You may as well tell me."

Charlotte leaned back in his arms and looked up at him. "Well, I know you'll say I shouldn't feel this way, but I still feel odd being in this house uninvited, sleeping in the master bedroom."

"I guess it's time you know the truth," Matt said quietly. "There's no reason for you to feel like an intruder here, Charlotte. This is my house."

She would have laughed if there hadn't been that sobering of his expression and unmistakable serious note in his voice. Yet even as she realized he wasn't joking, she couldn't truly believe what he had said. "What do you mean this is your house?" she asked.

"My grandfather left it to me. His grandfather, Jonathan Royall, was one of the first to discover silver in these mountains. He built the house and founded the town of Royal View. The mines played out eventually and were closed down, but the Royall family still owns property in the county."

Charlotte was stunned. Royall—Royal View. She had never imagined there could be a connection, and now she felt foolish, like a victim of a deliberate deceit. As if an oppressive weight had descended on her chest, she had trouble taking a breath. Her gaze was riveted on Matt's lean face. "That means the meadow is your property too, isn't it?" she asked weakly. When he nodded, she nearly groaned. "But why deceive me? Why aren't you even staying here instead of the lodge?"

"The lodge is more convenient, closer to all the sites. And, frankly, I didn't care for the thought of having Didi as a houseguest."

"But I still don't understand what you were trying to hide! Why didn't you tell me you own this house and the land?"

"Because I knew you'd react exactly the way you are," he replied grimly, reaching up to stroke her hair and sighing when she tensed. "At first there was no reason to tell you. And after we became more involved and I realized how badly you wanted me to choose this site for the airport, I knew you'd misunderstand my position if you knew I owned the land."

"Well, you're right. I don't understand your position at all. How can you be expected to make an unbiased decision about the airport when one of the possible sites is your own property? Talk about a conflict of interests. If the county commissioners knew about this—"

"Some of the commissioners have known me most of my life," Matt interrupted brusquely. "And all of them know I own this property. They chose the meadow as a possible site before even hiring me, and I'm giving it the same consideration as the others. Survey data and facts will make this decision, Charlotte."

"I wish I could believe that," she mumbled, sitting up in bed and clutching the bedclothes tightly around her. "But I think you and all the commissioners have known from the very beginning that the airport would be built on the plateau. You've told me yourself that it seems like the most suitable site."

"*Seems like* isn't good enough in civil engineering," Matt countered, a hard edge to his voice. Raising himself up, he leaned back against the headboard. "Engineering is a science. I can't look at a site and decide it 'seems' suitable. I have to prove it is."

"You can't want the airport to be built here though. That has to influence you," she argued bleakly, accepting the logic of what he had said yet unable to forget that he had deceived her for weeks. And if he had deceived her about his property, it was very possible that his tenderness tonight, his declaration that she was becoming very important to him, had been a deception too. Maybe he had simply sought the easiest way to get her into his bed. . . . She shook her head, pushing such devastating thoughts to the back of her mind. She couldn't think that he might have been using her the past few hours. If she considered that possibility now, she would probably start crying, and she refused to cry in front of him. Bending her head, she massaged the throbbing ache invading her temples. Then an unbidden thought intensified the aching. "Oh, God, Aunt Lou will be so hurt if she finds out who you really are."

"Little idiot, she knows who I am. She always has," Matt ground out between clenched teeth. One hand gripped her shoulder, and he turned her around, forcing her to meet his eyes. "Lou never lets anything slip by her, and she's sure as hell lived in this county long enough to know a Royall when she sees one. She knew I was one even before I told her my name. And it didn't seem to bother her a bit that I was to be the engineer in charge of this project. But then, she obviously has more faith in my professional integrity than you do. She doesn't automatically assume I'm going to cheat her."

More confused than ever, Charlotte could no longer sit still. Tossing back the covers, she slipped off the bed, then fought wildly to escape his hand when he caught her wrist in a viselike grip. Suddenly she was toppling back onto the mattress.

"Charlotte, for God's sake, get back in here," Matt muttered, one muscular arm going across her stomach to pin her down as he drew the bedclothes over her again. "You don't want to catch pneumonia, do you?"

All strength drained away and she went limp beneath his confining arm. Myriad conflicting emotions were bombarding her mind, and she no longer knew what to think of anything. If Aunt Lou trusted Matt, surely she could. Too weary to think rationally, she closed her eyes and didn't resist when Matt turned her over onto her side and began gently massaging her back and shoulders.

"We're both tired, Charlotte," he whispered, strong fingers loosening her tense muscles. "Let's go to sleep. We can discuss all this tomorrow and straighten everything out."

His hands felt too good, too coaxing; they strengthened her already desperate need to believe she could trust him. And she loved him so completely she almost had to.

Charlotte slept fitfully and awakened in the graying light of dawn. Turning her head on her pillow, she looked at Matt. His thick sandy hair had fallen forward to sweep across his forehead, and she wanted to gently brush it back. She didn't. Even asleep, he looked like a man who could be ruthless. Though his features were somewhat relaxed, the carved shape of his mouth and the firm line of his jaw made him look capable of taking whatever he wanted from life, regardless of the people he could hurt in the process. Or was her imagination simply working overtime? She didn't know.

Unable to fall asleep again, she slipped silently out of the bed. Since she knew now that this was Matt's house, she opened the closet and took out a navy flannel robe she found there, hurriedly putting it on. There was a great deal of robe and not a lot of Charlotte, but it was warm, and she wrapped it snugly around her. After putting another log on the dying fire with as little noise as possible, she walked to the window and gazed out at the snow which was falling less thickly this morning. The meadow and the rolling hills behind it were blanketed in white, and when she suddenly recalled something she had said to Matt the first time he had brought her out here, a dreadful fear stabbed her chest. She stood staring out, unable to move even when she heard Matt leave the bed and come toward her.

He wrapped his arms around her waist and drew her back against him as he murmured, "Why are you up so early?"

"It really does look like Vail, doesn't it?" she asked bluntly, ignoring his question and tensing in his embrace. "Maybe that's another reason you wouldn't want the airport here. I'm sure you'd make a great deal more money developing the land into a ski resort."

His arms tightened around her. "I have no intention of developing this land."

"Really?" She shook her head. "Why wouldn't you want to make all that money?"

"Because some things are more important than profits. And I wouldn't choose the plateau as the site for the airport if this meadow were more suitable." He spun her around to face him. "How do you think I could do that to you and your aunt?"

"Brad showed me exactly how capable some men are of forgetting people's feelings if they stand in the way of advancement," Charlotte retorted. "How do I know you aren't capable of hurting Aunt Lou for a considerable profit?"

His expression grew thunderous, his eyes stormy. "I'm tired of trying to convince you I'm not some sort of amoral profiteer," he muttered with a sweeping gesture of one hand toward the bed. "But answer this question, Charlotte. If you trust me so little, why did you let last night happen? Why did you let me be the first man to make love to you?"

Hurt and disillusionment made her defensive. She shrugged carelessly, heedless of the warning gleam in his eyes. "I'm twenty-three years old and I had to start somewhere, didn't I?" she taunted. "Why not with you? You're a very attractive man."

He moved with incredible speed to strip off her robe and sweep her up in his arms. "Well then, if it was nothing more than a learning experience, let's make sure your education's complete," he muttered, easily overcoming her efforts to escape him as he carried her to the bed. He dropped her onto the mattress and covered her slight body with his, catching her struggling hands in one of his and lifting them above her head.

"Matt, please, I didn't mean—" Charlotte's words

122

stuck in her throat as his hand feathered possessively over her. If he'd noticed the appeal in her wide eyes, he wasn't going to let it deter him. She trembled as his mouth hovered just above her own. "Don't do this. I don't want—"

"You do want me, just as much as I want you," he said roughly, and kissed her so thoroughly that her lips were soon clinging to his. He lifted his head to smile down at her. "You see, love? You're going to enjoy every minute of this."

CHAPTER SEVEN

Charlotte was determined not to respond. She tried to shrink into the mattress beneath her, but her lack of cooperation didn't discourage Matt. He actually seemed to accept it as something of a challenge, not taking by force what he could win by finesse. When Charlotte stiffened and pressed her lips tightly together during his next kiss, he gently turned her over onto her stomach and proceeded to press warm lingering kisses along every inch of her spine. He had never done that before, and Charlotte discovered to her shame that she wasn't at all immune to such an unexpected and unnerving caress. His firm lips were like a scorching brand that sent a rush of warmth through her lower limbs, and it took all her self-control and a great deal of pride for her to remain unyielding. But Matt was undaunted. His mouth sought the enticing arch of the small of her back and he followed the gentle curve of her rounded hips with his hand.

Charlotte lay very still, willing her muscles not to relax, yet she could do little to control the involuntary functions of her body, and her breathing accelerated enough for Matt to notice. With a muted murmur of satisfaction, he knelt astride her and commenced stroking her back with the expertise of a trained masseur.

You're not playing fair, she wanted to snap, but that admission would have been too revealing. Sheer mind control allowed her to remain rigid beneath his touch . . . until the kneading movements of his capable hands were punctuated by nibbling kisses followed by the feathering of his warm breath.

Appalled by the intensity of the thrill that shot through her, Charlotte bit down hard on her lower lip to keep from moaning aloud. With her face to one side on the pillow, she could peek out from beneath the thick fringe of her lashes and see him kneeling over her, and even that sight inflamed her senses. She watched the muscles in his arm and shoulder, and caught a glimpse of his chest, tapered waist, and the lean line of his hip when he shifted position. She squeezed her eyes tightly shut, but his image lingered clearly in her mind. Before she had any chance to make it vanish, Matt lifted her hair from her nape and touched firm lips to sensitized skin. A tremor fluttered deep within her, then ran visibly over her when he gently closed his teeth on the tender lobe of her exposed ear.

"Why are you fighting when you know how fantastic we can make each other feel?" he whispered provocatively.

Charlotte was weakening and he knew it. Clasping her narrow waist, he turned her back over, moving her legs outward to kneel between them. His hands glided up her sides to move in slow torturing circles over her breasts until the rosy peaks were aroused against his palms. The flame he ignited in Charlotte spread like wildfire, and when he lowered himself lightly on top of her, she was lost. A soft moan escaped her as she kissed him, and her hands drifted up to his bare shoulders. All resistance melted away and she became warmly acquiescent when he molded her supple body to his.

Matt's lips grazed over the curve of her slender neck, down to the shadowed hollow between her breasts. He cupped her breasts in his hands, kissing one nipple and the other, then took possession of her mouth once more, plundering the softness of her lips again and again. Charlotte's fingers tangled in his hair, then skimmed feverishly over his broad back. The heated surface of his skin was smooth, and she felt she could never get enough of touching him. When her slender legs intertwined with his, the extent of his desire became even more apparent.

"I want you," he murmured against her lips. "And you want me too, don't you, Charlotte?"

"Yes," she admitted. When he lifted his head, she opened her eyes, expecting to see a triumphant glint in his. Instead, she was mesmerized by the warm glow of tender indulgence she saw. She had never loved him more than she did in that moment. He held her gaze, watching her face as he slowly took her, and when a joyous smile trembled on her lips, he smiled back lazily.

With unhurried deliberation he introduced her to a fulfillment even more intense than he had given her before. Time and again he swept her tormentingly close to the peak of ecstasy then suddenly ceased moving, heightening her anticipation and pleasure when at last he took her to the crest and joined her there. He didn't let her go afterward, and she found she didn't want to let go of him. His shoulder became her pillow, and her arms lay lightly around his neck while his encircled her waist. She felt his breath stir her hair as he brushed a kiss across her temple just before she slept.

When Charlotte awoke later, Matt was still sleeping. With great care not to disturb him, she slipped from his embrace and out of the bed. After tossing his robe around her, she gathered up her clothes and went into the adjoining bathroom to take a shower. When she was finished and dressed, she found an unopened toothbrush in the cabinet above the wash basin and brushed her teeth. As she looked at her reflection in the mirror, the sudden memory of the night brought a pink glow to her cheeks. Yet a slight smile touched her lips. She couldn't be sorry for what had happened. She loved Matt, and her virginity had been part of her gift of love, one she didn't regret giving. And in the glow of the morning after, she refused to consider how much pain the future might bring if Matt never returned her love. He might even go away and never try to see her again, but right now he was nearby, asleep in the next room. For the moment that was all that mattered.

Charlotte left the bathroom quietly, tiptoed across the bedroom and down the stairs. In the clear light of day the house no longer seemed eerily strange, and she was able to truly appreciate its beauty and grace. Though it had probably been built in the Victorian era, its rooms were too spacious to qualify it as Victorian. It had a character all its own, as if that long-ago Royall had constructed his home the way he wanted it and not according to the popular style of his day. An independent man, no doubt, Charlotte thought with a smile, because independence was certainly a trait Matt had inherited from somebody.

In the kitchen Charlotte started coffee perking, then removed from the refrigerator some of the eggs and tomatoes her aunt had sent. While the coffee gurgled in the percolator, she went to a window and looked out. Snow still fell, but seemed to be tapering off to sparse flurries, which probably meant she and Matt would be able to get back to the lodge today. Absently twirling a strand of hair around one finger, she sighed deeply, knowing she shouldn't want to spend another night alone with Matt yet wanting exactly that.

Dragging herself away from the window and her disturbing thoughts, she went across the kitchen and found a tray. She didn't intend to serve Matt breakfast in bed, but she was going to take coffee up to him. Before she could take saucers and cups from a cupboard, however, Matt walked into the kitchen, clad in the robe she had worn earlier. Charlotte couldn't prevent her gaze from wandering along the brown V of skin exposed where the shawl collar came together across his chest, down to his hair-roughened legs and bare feet. Even his feet were attractive, she thought, and laughed mentally at herself. Only a woman in love would notice a man had nice feet. She pretended she was looking at them for an altogether different reason. "Going around without shoes in weather like this isn't a good idea," she stated matter-of-factly. "You could catch a cold."

Matt came toward her. "Would you care if I did?"

"Of course. You'd probably take to your bed at the

lodge and I'd have to play nursemaid to you. I've heard young men can be impossible patients."

"How hard-hearted you pretend to be," he said, smiling knowingly as he placed his hands around her waist. He drew her slightly closer and his smile faded. "Charlotte, you wouldn't listen to me before, but are you willing to listen to reason now?"

Putting her own hands on top of his, to hold them around her, she answered candidly, "Matt, I'm afraid reason flies out the window for me the moment you walk in the door."

"Why is that, Charlotte?" he asked, his eyes narrowing speculatively. "Because of the attraction between us?"

"Maybe that's part of it." That and a great deal of love, she added mentally, then lifted her shoulders in a weary shrug. "But mostly it's this damned airport project. I don't want to see Aunt Lou lose everything, and you're the person who'll decide whether she does or not. So to learn that you own this property and might have your own reason to recommend the plateau—"

"I have no intention of developing any of the land I own," Matt cut in sternly. "It would be nice if you could believe that, but I'm tired of trying to convince you. Besides, I think it's important for you to decide you can trust me on your own."

Or maybe he just didn't care enough to keep trying to win her trust, Charlotte thought bleakly, staring at the broad implacable line of his back when he released her abruptly and walked past her to pour the coffee.

Within a week the snow melted away in a brief and unexpected spell of warm weather. In the two weeks that followed, Matt and his crew finished surveying all the sites and Charlotte was hard-pressed to keep up with her own free-lance work and the site drawings she was doing for Matt. On the Friday he sent the crew back to the home office in Denver, Charlotte still had the last two drawings to do, so they worked together all day and into the evening to finish both of them. With the last stroke of her pencil, the dread Charlotte had been warding off for days settled like a lump in her chest. Except for deciding which site he would recommend to the county commissioners, Matt was now finished with the preliminary phase of the airport project. Nothing further could be done until spring, and though he hadn't mentioned leaving the lodge, she knew he would soon have to return to Denver. Watching him as he glanced over the drawing she had just done, she had to wonder if he would even give her a second thought after he left.

She wouldn't think that way as long as he was still here, she decided with a resolute squaring of her shoulders, but when he looked up from the drawing at her, the smile she gave him was strained.

"You're tired, aren't you?" he asked softly, placing his drawing and hers into a portfolio on the desk. He went to the bar and returned to hand her a glass of white wine, then pulled her out of her chair and directed her to the sofa. He sat down beside her, stretching his long legs out before him as he took a sip of his own Scotch and water. With his free hand he massaged the back of his neck. "It has been a hectic two weeks. I'm sorry you haven't had much time to relax."

"You had to finish before it snowed again. I understand that," said Charlotte. There was some hesitancy in her voice when she went on to ask a question she really didn't want to ask. "Now that you have all the data about the sites, when . . . will you tell us your decision?"

"I don't think I like the way you phrased that," he replied somewhat mockingly. "Almost as if you think I've already made the decision, when I've told you repeatedly that I haven't."

"But—"

"Charlotte, hush," he commanded in a whisper, pressing a finger against her lips. His hand slipped down to encircle her neck as he shook his head. "You know we simply go around in circles when we discuss this subject, and I don't want to argue about it again, especially tonight. And I don't think you want to either. Do you?"

"Well no, but—" This time a kiss silenced her, and she was almost relieved, because he was right about their arguments getting them nowhere. Besides, she was feeling unusually vulnerable and insecure, and his arms around her diminished those feelings.

When he took the wineglass from her hand to put it on the table beside her, she didn't protest, and went willingly as he then pulled her close against him. Though she sometimes felt she should be ashamed of her need to be with him when she had so many doubts about him, she was coming to the realization that this was a need too basic and strong to be controlled. Her love for him was too powerful. A few minutes later,

131

when he turned off the lights and led her upstairs, it would have been pointless to even pretend to herself that she didn't want to go with him.

For the first three nights after Matt and Charlotte had returned to the lodge after staying at his house, she had slept in her own room. On the fourth evening, however, when Lou had retired for the night, leaving the two of them alone downstairs, the inevitable had happened. Matt had taken Charlotte to bed with him. Because neither of them cared for the idea of her sneaking in and out of his room, she had stayed until morning. After that it had seemed natural and right for her to spend every night with him. And she wasn't ashamed of that. She loved Matt and desperately needed to be with him. She didn't even make a concerted effort to hide the arrangement from Lou. Yet she didn't advertise it either, and if her aunt had noticed she no longer slept in her own room, she had given no indication of it.

Now, as Charlotte and Matt entered his room, she simply felt she belonged there. While he took a quick shower, she removed a nightgown from a drawer she had commandeered, stripped off her clothes, and slipped it on over her head. She sat down before the vanity mirror and began brushing her hair. A few minutes later, when Matt left the bathroom and came across the room to stand behind her, she smiled at his reflection. He took the brush from her hand. Lifting a golden swath of her hair, he slipped the bristles through the silken strands and his knuckles faintly brushed against her nape. Charlotte felt weak with the delightful warmth that swept over her when he pushed her hair aside and bent down to graze his lips down

132

the side of her neck. Through lowered lashes she watched him in the mirror. His bare torso gleamed in the dim lamplight, and his sandy hair was damp from the shower. When she lifted a hand to run her fingers through it, he drew her up from her chair and into his arms.

Matt's desire for Charlotte had lost none of its feverish intensity in the weeks they had been lovers. Knowing wild forceful passion simmered just beneath the surface in him, and knowing she had the ability to unleash that wild force, was a spellbinding fascination that always heightened her own response. Tonight was no different. Although he was as gentle with her as he had ever been, he at last took his own satisfaction with a fierce conquering demand that made the giving as wonderously pleasurable as the taking. Later, after they had exchanged many lazy kisses of complete fulfillment, Charlotte lay in the circle of his arm, delighting simply in being near him. Unfortunately the delight faded and apprehension took its place too soon.

"I'm going to have to leave for Denver early in the morning," Matt said sleepily as he trailed his hand over her upper arm. "I hadn't planned to go, but when the office phoned today, I was told the supervisor of one of my other projects is having some problems he wants to discuss with me."

"Oh, I see," Charlotte murmured, managing to keep her voice from sounding choked, despite the tightening constriction that had attacked her throat. "Well, I can understand why it was so important for us to finish the site drawings tonight. Of course, you'll have to take them with you."

"I probably will take them, but I don't have to,"

Matt corrected matter-of-factly. "I'm coming back Tuesday because I want to evaluate all the data and make my decision here. If I decide to recommend the plateau as the site, I'll tell Lou myself. I feel I should do that much for her."

"Yes. Yes, I guess so. Then we'll expect you back Tuesday," Charlotte answered woodenly, wanting with all her heart to believe he would return, but afraid she would be playing the fool if she did. Maybe this was simply his way of walking away from their relationship.

A few minutes later, when Matt's breathing had slowed and become more even, Charlotte knew he was asleep. Her entire body went cold, then hot, then icy cold again, and she could not prevent the tears that had been building behind her eyes from flowing over to spill down her cheeks. Determined to make no sound, she pressed her lips tightly together and impatiently wiped the tears away with the back of her hand. She stared into the darkness, wondering if this was the last night she would ever spend with Matt.

The three days that followed were the loneliest Charlotte had ever endured. To keep from moping around the lodge, she never allowed herself to be still a moment during the days. There was always something to be done, but even such hectic activity didn't make the nights more peaceful. She didn't sleep very well, and by Tuesday she was tired and upset enough to flinch every time the phone in the lodge rang. Each time, she feared it would be Matt calling to say he couldn't come back.

Matt didn't call, however. About two o'clock Charlotte heard the fine-tuned purr of a powerful car engine, and it sounded so similar to Matt's BMW that her heart skipped several beats before beginning to thud wildly. She stood by the desk in the public room, unable to move until she heard a car door slam, then widely spaced footfalls on the porch. She compulsively smoothed her hair, and when the door opened and Matt came in, she felt dizzy with relief. A smile lit up her face and she started across the room toward him, but something in his expression stopped her. Something was terribly wrong—she could see it in his eyes and face. There were grim lines of strain around his mouth that she had never seen before, and this time dread instead of hope made her heart stop for an instant.

When Matt came to her and gently kissed her lips, she was glad, yet the gesture couldn't eradicate the fear rising in her. "You look . . . upset," she said haltingly, hesitantly putting her hands to his arms. "What's wrong? What is it?"

He touched her hair and didn't answer immediately. "I had more free time than I expected in Denver, so I looked over the site drawings and data for the airport," he began after a moment, his deep voice almost devoid of expression. "There were reports members of my crew had prepared that I'd never gone over, and before I read them, I hoped I'd discover my professional instincts had been wrong. But I didn't, Charlotte. The plateau seemed like the most suitable site to me because it is. All the information we gathered up here makes that very clear."

"You mean you've made your decision?" she exclaimed softly. "But Matt, you can't—"

"Charlotte, the facts say everything, and I can't change them," he interrupted gently, slipping his hand around the back of her neck. "The plateau's long and wide and fairly flat. The substratum rock provides the best possible foundation. All the other sites except the meadow are a great deal smaller, but the meadow is flooded an average of two times a year, and sometimes the water stands on it for two to three days. There's just no getting around it—the plateau is by far the most suitable site."

Though Charlotte had tried to prepare herself for the worst possible news, she was still disappointed. "I guess I hoped you really wouldn't go through with it," she said almost inaudibly. "Naive of me, wasn't it?"

"I couldn't even call myself a civil engineer if I hadn't chosen such an obvious site. You can try to blame me and suspect my motives, but somewhere in the back of your mind I think you know I only did what I had to do."

"I don't know anything anymore. That's my problem. But that's not my main concern right now," Charlotte said dully. "I'm more worried about how to break the news to Aunt Lou."

"I made the decision, so I'll tell her myself," Matt declared, his tone leaving no room for argument. "I do think you should be with her, though."

Agreeing, Charlotte left him to go upstairs and get her aunt, who was cleaning one of the bedrooms. Although Charlotte dragged her feet every step of the way, she and Louisa were back downstairs much too soon. They sat together on the sofa while Matt took a nearby chair.

Mercifully, he didn't beat around the bush or make

136

excuses. Forthright yet kind, he simply stated his decision. His honest respect for Lou and a genuine tone of regret softened the blow a bit, and for that Charlotte was grateful to him. Whatever his true motivation for chosing the plateau, she thought, at least he wasn't completely indifferent to her aunt's feelings.

As for Louisa, she said nothing for several moments, but a light went out of her eyes and her face fell. "Well, that's that, isn't it? You've both been trying to tell me this might happen, and now it has," she finally replied, controlling a quaver in her voice with heroic effort. Slowly, she rubbed the palms of her hands over the skirt of her apron and rose to her feet to stand straight and proud. "If you two will excuse me, I have to go put more seed in the bird feeders."

Watching Louisa walk out through the kitchen, Charlotte felt tears filling her eyes. Unable to look at Matt, she stared instead at his feet. There was no recrimination, only desolate acceptance in her tone when she did speak. "Well, I guess all the landowners in the county will be pleased. They'll have their airport exactly where they've wanted it."

"I'm a landowner, and I'm far from pleased. But I made the only decision I could." Matt stood and reached down to take both Charlotte's hands to draw her up before him. A finger lifted her chin. "I regret this as much as you do. I don't think anyone in the county ever wanted to see Lou hurt."

"I'm sure they didn't," Charlotte answered stiffly. "Maybe that'll give her some comfort when the bulldozers start rolling past here. But I doubt it."

"So do I, but some things can't be helped," said Matt, his voice taking on a harder edge, as if his patience were growing thin. As his dark gaze drifted over her face, however, he sighed and began massaging her shoulders comfortingly. "Look, I understand you're upset. It only makes sense for you to be worried about Lou. I suppose you'll be staying with her awhile longer, until she's had some time to accept the situation."

"Yes, I'll stay awhile. But your job here is through until spring, isn't it?" Charlotte murmured, unhappiness for Louisa and herself darkening her green eyes as she looked at him. "I'm sure you have a great deal to do in Denver now."

"Too much, unfortunately. In fact, the supervisor I mentioned the other day is having so many problems with his project that I have to get back to Denver today," Matt explained. "I'd planned to stay here through the weekend to make the decision about the airport, but since I've already made it, I can't neglect this problem with the other project. I'll be back Friday evening or Saturday morning at the latest. I'm sorry to bring such bad news and then leave right away, but you understand, don't you?"

She nodded, feeling as if powerful relentless fingers had gripped her heart and were squeezing. She understood all right. He was going back to Denver today, and she doubted seriously that he would return Friday or Saturday. This was the way so many relationships ended. Promises were made but not kept until finally the promiser just drifted away and what had been was over forever. At least she knew the rules before the game began; she wouldn't have to endure the disappointment when Saturday morning came and he didn't appear. Actually, she had no one except herself to blame for the hurt she was experiencing now. When she had first met Matt, she suspected that his involvements with women meant far less to him than his career. Foolishly she had hoped his relationship with her could develop into something much more meaningful, something lasting. Well, she had gambled and lost, she told herself, but now wasn't the time to dwell on that. After Matt left, she would have nothing but empty time in which to put the pieces of her life back together. With all these thoughts bombarding her brain, she found it impossible to even force a tiny smile for Matt's benefit. She could only look blindly up at him, her face expressionless.

"Well, the sooner I get back to Denver, the sooner I can take care of the supervisor's problems," Matt said with a quick glance at his wristwatch.

When he pulled Charlotte close and his lips descended on hers, she felt such a piercing sense of loss that she couldn't prevent herself from kissing him back. After he released her, she walked to the door with him.

He glanced back over his shoulder on the way out. "Friday or Saturday, then."

"Yes," she answered automatically, while misery welled inside her. It was no longer a case of his letting her down easy. Now he was merely prolonging the agony, and she was almost relieved when he got into his car, waved good-bye, and drove away.

The next morning all Charlotte's worst fears were realized. Guests were due to arrive at the lodge the next day, and Louisa was bustling around the kitchen, checking her food supply. Suddenly she gasped, clutched at her chest, and sank down onto the floor near the counter. With lightning speed Charlotte was across the room, sheer necessity preventing her from panicking. Kneeling beside Lou, she noticed the bluish tinge of her lips and the beaded perspiration on her forehead. Knowing what those two symptoms could mean, Charlotte quickly undid the top three buttons of her aunt's gingham dress, but that did little to help the woman in her ragged attempts to catch her breath. Still conscious, her face twisted by the severe pain in her chest, she stared up at Charlotte, whose cool calm expression belied the inner turmoil churning in her stomach.

"Let me help you sit up a little. I read somewhere that that might ease the pain," she said gently. Snatching a cushion from one of the wooden kitchen chairs, she slipped it behind her aunt as she eased her up to rest back against the cabinets. While Louisa's breathing became less labored and some of the strain left her lined face, Charlotte found a bottle of tiny pills in her aunt's apron pocket, and as the doctor had told her to do in an emergency, placed one in Louisa's mouth. "Now I'm going to call for the ambulance, but that will only take a second and I'll be right back."

While awaiting the arrival of help, Charlotte could only try to make Louisa as comfortable as possible. She had never felt so relieved in her life as she did when she finally heard the distant whine of a siren. A few minutes later she led the ambulance attendants into the kitchen. After propping Louisa up against pillows on the stretcher because she couldn't lie flat, they carried her outside and rushed her away. In her Omni Charlotte kept pace with the ambulance ahead, though under normal circumstances she would have been petrified taking the hairpin curves at such a breakneck speed.

At the small hospital in Juniper, Charlotte paced back and forth in the waiting area until Dr. Sommers finally appeared. His grim expression made her feel nauseous, and she clenched her hands so tightly that her nails dug into her palms.

"We're not equipped to handle Louisa's condition here," he began without ceremony. "I want to take her to the airport in Steamboat Springs and fly her to Denver in my plane. I'll get someone else to fly it so I can keep a close eye on her during the flight. She's agreed to go."

"Denver? To the medical center? But Boulder's closer and—"

"The medical center will be much better. They have the best cardiologists and facilities. And Louisa's going to need them."

"Her condition is very bad then, isn't it?" Charlotte asked weakly, beginning to tremble.

"The prognosis is poor. But there's hope if she gets the proper care soon," he replied briskly, though kindliness warmed his eyes. "All I can say definitely is that she can't remain here, we don't have the facilities she needs. So I'm flying her to Denver immediately. I'm sure you want to go with her, but I'm afraid you'll have to drive there. I have a four-seater plane, but it's been equipped with removable rear seats to accommodate a stretcher in an emergency."

"I understand. I'll drive to Denver. You just take care of Aunt Lou," Charlotte said quickly. "Tell her I'll be with her by this evening."

Patting her shoulder reassuringly, Dr. Sommers nodded and returned to his patient. For a long moment after he left, Charlotte stood staring down, the tears swimming in her eyes blurring the scrolled pattern of the carpet. When she thought she was sufficiently composed again, she left the hospital and started back to the lodge to pack, and to arrange for other lodgings for the guests due that weekend.

An hour later Charlotte was driving to Denver. The doctor's words echoed in her head, and her fears for her aunt were mounting. Hoping to divert her thoughts, she turned on the radio, but the lively music and the announcer's constant chatter soon became unnerving and she switched it off.

A desolate sigh escaped her as she involuntarily remembered how comforting Matt had been during the earlier, less serious crisis with her aunt. Although she knew even thinking about him only caused her considerable pain, she couldn't help it. She was filled with an aching need to have him beside her now.

CHAPTER EIGHT

Charlotte spent two nights in a Denver motel before deciding that arrangement was far too expensive. On Friday morning she checked out and took up her vigil in the solarium near the cardiac care unit in the medical center. By sleeping on one of the sofas there whenever she could, and eating downstairs in the cafeteria, she figured she could hold out for a couple of days and nights before sheer weariness would force her to return to the lodge. After that she thought she could drive back to Denver every other day at least, though she was only allowed to visit Louisa for five minutes every couple of hours.

Louisa's doctor was running her through a gauntlet of tests, and though Charlotte knew every procedure was necessary, the constant poking and prodding seemed to weaken her aunt, etching deeper lines of weariness in her face. Charlotte felt completely helpless and lonely. Her parents were touring China and she hadn't been able to track them down yet, so Charlotte had to face these critical first days alone. It was to her that Louisa's doctor came with frighteningly grim test results, and the successive barrages of bad news took a heavy toll on her. Charlotte felt constantly on the verge of tears. Sometimes she could escape her mounting anxiety by talking to other people who waited in the solarium, but it wasn't the same as having someone with her who loved Louisa as much as she did.

By Friday evening Louisa's doctor had decided a heart bypass operation was her only chance for survival, and worse yet, that she was at present too weak to undergo the surgery. They would have to wait until she regained some of her strength. After asking the doctor a few pertinent questions, Charlotte didn't detain him further, knowing he had many other patients. When he was gone, she tried to remember that heart surgery was a miracle of modern medicine, one that saved many lives, but all the same, it was terrifying to know her aunt's condition was so serious that it warranted such extreme treatment.

Unable to stop worrying, Charlotte flipped through outdated magazines until well past midnight. Alone now in the solarium, she went into the rest room to wash her face and brush her teeth, then came back out and chose one of the corner sofas as her bed for the night. She curled up on the cushions and pulled her coat over her, but within a minute she was turning onto her other side, trying to shield her eyes from the everpresent light in the corridor. When she finally did drop off to sleep, it was only to awaken at frequent intervals, and she soon realized that a hospital wasn't quiet at night. There were muffled sounds of activity, loud whispers, and the muted rush of rubber soles along tiled corridors. Consequently, she didn't rest well at all. By the time morning finally arrived, her eyes felt gritty from lack of sleep and she was too tired to bother with breakfast, so she simply had coffee in the snack bar. After a short walk outside in the brisk morning air, she returned to the solarium, shunned the magazines, and instead went to stand before one of the huge plate-glass windows. Providing a spectacular western backdrop, the Rockies rose up from the plain to stand like sentinels over the city. In spots, white clouds laced the mountain peaks, accentuating their splendor and adding to their primeval mystique. The lure of the Rocky Mountains was almost magical to Charlotte, and the beauty of the panoramic scene beckoned to her. Unshed tears stung the back of her eyes as she gazed out the window, wishing she and Louisa were together at the lodge at that moment.

A hand suddenly descended on Charlotte's right shoulder, and she tensed, afraid it would be the doctor with more bad news. A knot formed in the pit of her stomach as she turned around, and when she saw Matt towering over her, a scowl on his face, there was a revealing hitch in her sharply drawn breath.

"Oh, hi," she said, fighting the desire to throw herself into his arms. Slipping her hands into the pockets of her corduroy pants, she looked up at him. "What brings you here?"

"Why the hell didn't you call me Wednesday, when you got to Denver?" he asked, his voice deceptively calm. He grasped her upper arms as if he intended to give her a good shaking, but instead, he simply glowered down at her, his tawny eyes narrowed and glinting. "You've been here three days and you haven't even tried to get in touch with me? Would you care to tell me why? I must have tried to call the lodge twenty times this morning to tell you I couldn't get back up there this weekend, and when I never got an answer, I thought something might be wrong. So I phoned that gossipy postmistress in Royal View. Imagine my surprise when she told me Dr. Sommers flew Lou here Wednesday and that you had been here since then. For God's sake, Charlotte, why didn't you let me know you were in town?"

"Well, you did tell me how very busy you'd be. And you obviously still are, since you weren't going to get back to the lodge today either," she answered, barely able to mask her sarcasm as she met his gaze directly. "I didn't want to bother you while you were having so many problems with that other project."

"That's the most ridiculous answer I've ever heard," he said. "But I suppose I'm getting this cold shoulder because you blame me for Lou being here in the first place, right? Her heart attack is the direct result of telling her my decision about the site. Isn't that what you think?"

"Well, the idea has crossed my mind," Charlotte conceded tersely, her green eyes flashing with defiance and resentment. "It is quite a coincidence that she had the attack the day after you told her you'd chosen the plateau as the airport site."

"I don't imagine my decision improved her health any," he muttered roughly. "I'm sorry for that. But I don't think you can logically blame me because the lodge happens to be close to the most suitable site."

"Oh, what difference does all that make now?" Charlotte muttered, weariness and her delayed reaction at seeing Matt again beginning to make her tremble. Withdrawing a shaky hand from one pocket, she pressed her fingers against her forehead. "What's the

146

use of brooding about what caused Aunt Lou's attack? Now all that matters is her getting well again."

"Now you're beginning to make sense," he said bluntly, then relented, his hands on her gentling. "How is she? Obviously, since Sommers brought her here, her condition is very serious."

With a nod Charlotte repeated what the doctor had told her last night. There was a definite quaver in her voice when she added, "So they'll do the surgery when her condition has stabilized and her electrolytes or something like that are balanced. Then her chances of survival will be higher. But I hate the thought of her having to go through such an ordeal at any time."

"I know you do," Matt said understandingly. Moving closer, he brushed light fingertips over the faint violet crescents that lay beneath her eyes. "But I'm sure Lou doesn't want you worrying about her so much that you get sick too. You look exhausted, Charlotte. I bet you've spent every day here, haven't you?"

"What else could I do? Since I can only see Aunt Lou for a few minutes every couple of hours, I have to stay and see her whenever I can."

"Have you seen her this morning?" Matt asked. When she shook her head, he added, "That's good. If Lou sees you the way you look right now, she's only going to start worrying about you not taking care of yourself. And that she doesn't need."

"I'm sure I can't look all that bad," Charlotte muttered defensively, combing her fingers through her hair, hoping to fluff it a bit. "I'm fine, really, just a little tired."

"You're so worn out I can feel you shaking," Matt argued, taking both her hands in his. "I want you to go back to your hotel right now and get a few hours of sleep. You can have a nurse tell Lou why you're not here. Then early this afternoon, after I'm finished at the office and you've gotten some rest, I'll take you to lunch somewhere. When you see Lou later today, you'll be much more relaxed."

"I'd rather just stay here," Charlotte murmured, unwilling to accept the sympathy and support he obviously felt obligated to offer. "I mean, it's kind of you to invite me out to lunch but—"

"I wouldn't call it an invitation. It's actually an order," he cut in, his expression as stern as the authoritative note in his low voice. "You need to rest this morning, and you're going to. So get your coat and I'll drop you by your hotel on my way to the office."

When he started to draw her away from the window, Charlotte hung back, shaking her head. "Actually, I'm not staying in a hotel."

"Where then? Which motel?"

"Well, I did stay two nights at one near here, but it was getting expensive. . . . So," she gestured hesitantly, "I decided to spend last night in here."

Matt uttered several explicit curses quietly enough so that only she could hear. A reaction that far surpassed mere impatience made his face a hard bronzed mask, and he jerked her toward him. His hands released hers only to grasp her waist. "You must be the most stubborn person alive," he exclaimed. "It's ridiculous enough that you didn't call me as soon as you came to Denver, but for you to try to rough it by sleeping in the solarium! Dammit, wasn't that carrying resentment a little too far? You could have at least

148

called and told me you were short of money. I owe you some anyway."

Charlotte flinched. Her face went pale. "You don't owe me anything," she said raspingly. "I didn't sleep with you for—"

"My God, you could try the patience of a saint," he muttered, exasperation brightening the glint in his eyes. "Do you get some kind of satisfaction out of deliberately misunderstanding what I say? You know damned well I didn't mean I owed you money for the time we spent together in bed. I owe you for the drawings you did."

"Oh. Those," she said weakly, embarrassment rushing warm color into her cheeks again. "I didn't think about the drawings. But I don't want any money for them. I refuse to profit from anything remotely connected to that horrendous airport project."

"All right by me. I wasn't planning to let you check into another motel anyway. That's not much better than camping out here." He bent down and swept Charlotte's belongings up from the sofa beside him. After he handed her purse to her, he draped her coat around her shoulders, ignoring her muffled protest. "You'll be more comfortable staying at my house while Lou's in the hospital. Let's go. I'll drive you out there now."

She shook her head. "No thanks. I might get emergency calls in the middle of the night, and I wouldn't think of inconveniencing you that way."

"Charlotte, be careful," Matt warned, his voice low, his expression menacing. "Do you want to walk out of here with some dignity or shall I toss you over my shoulder and carry you out?"

She couldn't dismiss his threat. Something in his demeanor made her suspect he just might be capable of carrying it out. Suddenly all the fight left her and she recognized her overwhelming susceptibility to him. She took a deep tremulous breath. "Don't harass me, Matt, please," she whispered. "I just want to stay here. And I'm so tired. . . ."

"Too tired to stay. That's what I've been trying to tell you," he declared, pulling her closer by the lapels of her coat, then holding it expectantly until she surrendered and slipped her arms into the sleeves. He led her out into the corridor, then stopped by cardiac care's nurses' station, where he soon had a starched and capped young woman promising faithfully to tell Lou that Charlotte wouldn't be able to visit her until that afternoon.

Matt insisted Charlotte leave her car in the medical center parking lot, and that quickly proved to be a wise decision. In the luxurious comfort of his BMW she couldn't prevent herself from curling up in the seat, and immediately commenced a losing battle with her heavy eyelids. When a traffic light stopped them a few minutes later, her eyes did flicker open once, and she saw they were headed west out of town, toward the mountains.

The drive to Matt's house took no more than twenty minutes, and when he stroked a hand over her hair to awaken her from her brief nap, she responded groggily, feeling very disoriented. He had parked the car in a curved graveled driveway in front of a lovely old two-story brick house. He opened the door on the passenger side and she got out to gaze drowsily at the white columned portico, gracefully wide bay windows, and streamers of dark green ivy that festooned the outer walls. It was a beautiful house, but Charlotte had no idea what route he had taken to get them there. All she knew was that she was now in the western outskirts of Denver, because the Rockies loomed closer than they had in the city. She glanced sideways at Matt as he unlocked the heavy oak front door, and the sight of his hard profile did nothing to still the odd uneasiness she was feeling.

Opening the door, Matt indicated with a gesture that she should precede him. She stepped into a wide hall where light filtering through stained glass windows danced in a rainbow of colors on a buffed and gleaming hardwood floor.

"How lovely," she murmured, then sleepily returned his indulgent smile. "That must not have sounded very enthusiastic, but I meant it. I'm just feeling groggy."

"I noticed," he answered wryly, taking her hand to lead her toward a curving staircase. "What you most definitely need is a few hours in bed."

Though the words weren't meant to be provocative, they reminded her that they hadn't discussed the sleeping arrangements. "Which spare room will you give me?" she began diplomatically. "In a house as big as this, you must have several."

Matt's eyebrows lifted. Yet if he had assumed she would sleep in his room, he made no mention of it. "There are four spare bedrooms," he said, with what seemed a trace of amusement tugging upward at his lips. He slipped an arm around Charlotte's waist and guided her up the steps. "So I'll let you choose the one you want."

"That's okay. You decide. As long as it has a bed."

Taking her at her word, Matt took her into the first bedroom along the upstairs corridor. "I'll bring your suitcase up from the car, then go on to the office," he said. "You just sleep while I'm gone. I'll wake you when I get back, between one thirty and two."

After he had brought up her luggage and left her alone in the house, Charlotte stood in the middle of the room to undress. Though she was usually a very tidy person, this time she allowed herself to leave her things where they fell on the floor. She padded into the adjoining bathroom. Sure she would fall asleep in the tub, she settled for a hot shower instead, put on a nightgown, and went straight to bed.

As Charlotte slept, she drifted through a series of happy dreams. In one Aunt Lou was healthy again, and the lodge's serenity wasn't being threatened by progress. It was spring and Charlotte was visiting, but not alone. Matt was with her and there were no problems or disagreements forming a barrier between them. In her dream, Charlotte's love for Matt was returned and she was filled with joy and contentment. They smiled at each other a great deal. It was the kind of dream that one wants never to end, and when it began to fade away as she started to waken, she wanted to sink back into deep sleep again to retain it. For a moment it seemed she had succeeded. Matt was softly saying her name and she felt a feather-light kiss on her forehead. Even when she opened her eyes slightly and realized Matt was actually there, sitting on the bed beside her, the effects of the dream still held sway. Warm and soft and drowsily seductive, she looked up at him and ran a hand along his arm.

152

Through his shirt-sleeve she felt his powerful muscles harden with her caressing touch. The light cover over her outlined the slender length of her body, and Matt's narrowing gaze roamed slowly over her. When his eyes sought hers again, she gave him a little smile that was beckoning yet somewhat shy too.

"Kiss me," she whispered. "Please, Matt." When he leaned down, she slipped her arms from beneath the bedcovers to glide them across his shoulders. His lips touched hers, then parted them with swift possessive force. She moaned faintly as his arms came around her and he gathered her roughly to him.

"Charlotte, I've missed holding you like this," he murmured huskily between devouring kisses that ravished her mouth. He slid a hand beneath the soft curtain of her shimmering hair, his fingers grazing the sensitive skin of her nape. As she seemed to melt against him, he arched her back slightly over his supporting arms and his lips continued the conquering assault on her senses, blazing a fiery path along the line of her jaw into the slight hollows beneath her cheekbones and even over closed, softly fringed eyelids. Charlotte couldn't think rationally, nor did she want to. Still caught up in the magic of her dream, she couldn't resist Matt. It seemed so right to be with him, and her arms went around his waist, her hands on his back urging him closer. His groan was muffled in the scented thickness of her hair as he swiftly lowered himself onto the bed, his weight pressing her into the yielding springiness of the mattress and holding her captive. His mouth took hers again, coaxing her lips apart. Yet when he allowed his hand to drift down over her full firm breasts, his touch burning her skin through the thin gown, and she breathed his name, he suddenly tensed and lifted his head.

"You still sound tired," he murmured when she opened her eyes to look at him. He moved over onto his side to play idly with a tendril of her hair. "I want you, but this isn't the time. When you've had a chance to get enough rest, and those shadows under your eyes are gone . . ." His words trailed away, and he swung himself off the bed to walk across the room without a backward glance. "Get dressed and we'll go someplace quiet for lunch before I take you to see Lou."

As he pulled the door shut on his way out, Charlotte passed a shaky hand over her eyes and tried to will away the constricting pain knotting in her chest. But it remained as she wondered bleakly if he had only used her weariness as an excuse to reject what she offered so willingly. Perhaps even his physical need for her was starting to wane.

Staying at Matt's house made the following days less hectic. Though Charlotte still spent long hours in the solarium at the medical center, she was less tense knowing she no longer had to sleep overnight on the sofa or return to a motel room nearly as sterile as the hospital. And she didn't feel so alone anymore either, because Matt was being very supportive. Charlotte suspected he might be feeling guilty because of the decision he had made about the airport project, but if guilt was his motivation for being exceptionally kind, it didn't matter to her. She needed him too badly to question his reason for standing by her. It was such a relief to have someone to talk to and lean on.

By Sunday evening the staff had become so accustomed to seeing Matt with Charlotte, that the resident on duty in cardiac care approached him instead of her as they were leaving Louisa's bedside.

"Our chief cardiologist, Dr. Nathan, wants to see both of you in his office right away," the resident said. "Turn right down this hall and it's the third door on your left. If he's not in, call his service and he'll get back to you—he said he had to speak to you tonight."

Charlotte's eyes, suddenly wide with apprehension, darted up to Matt's face, and she found some comfort in the fact that his calm expression didn't change at all. After he thanked the resident for the message, he led her by the hand into the corridor and didn't release her even when he knocked on Dr. Nathan's door and a voice bade them enter. The chief cardiologist's outer office was deserted and dark, but a light shone through a doorway behind the reception desk. Matt squeezed Charlotte's hand reassuringly as they entered the doctor's domain.

A small pudgy man with silver hair, Dr. Nathan nodded in greeting then rose from his swivel chair. His long white coat flapped about his knees when he came around his desk to shake Matt's hand. Waving them both into chairs, he leaned back against the desk's edge and stared silently at Charlotte for a moment.

"Dr. Michaels called me in on your aunt's case this morning, Ms. Jordan," he declared abruptly. "I believe he has discussed the surgery we plan to do?"

Charlotte nodded. "He explained it to me, yes."

"Fine. That's good," the doctor muttered absently, slipping a gold fountain pen into his shirt pocket. "Well, I had to see you this evening because I decided to schedule the surgery for tomorrow morning."

"Tomorrow!" Charlotte gasped, color draining from her cheeks. She clutched the arms of her chair so tightly, her knuckles were white. "But why so soon? I thought Aunt Lou had to be stronger before you operated."

"She's not as strong as I'd like her to be," Dr. Nathan conceded. "Though her condition in general has improved somewhat, she's still very weak. But after examining her this morning, I have to concur with Dr. Michaels. We're going to have to risk the surgery now. Her ventricular function is deteriorating more rapidly than Michaels had anticipated, and we feel we should operate as soon as possible."

"Oh, God," Charlotte cried, the tremor that shook her entire body lessening slightly when Matt touched her shoulder. She looked at Dr. Nathan beseechingly. "But if she's still weak, what . . . what are her chances?"

"I don't like to give odds, especially when they wouldn't be very good ones," the doctor answered truthfully, allowing his professional demeanor to slip away and compassion to show through. "I'm sorry to have to give you news like this, Ms. Jordan, but I felt you should know. We'll do our best, of course, but considering her age and the damage done . . ."

"I understand. And I do appreciate your telling me everything." Still noticeably pale, Charlotte stood when Matt did, and clutched his hand. She left it to him to say good-bye to the doctor, yet as they started toward the open door, she stopped abruptly and looked back. "What time tomorrow, Dr. Nathan?"

"Eight o'clock was the earliest I could book O.R. on such short notice. If you can get here some time before seven, you should be able to see her, but only for a few minutes."

Nodding, Charlotte bit down hard on her lower lip and hurried out of his office, easily able to keep up with Matt's long strides. Knowing he was looking down at her, she tried valiantly to stop her chin from wobbling, but it was a futile attempt. She was very close to bursting into a storm of tears, and he was wise enough to remain silent and give her a chance to regain control of her overwrought emotions. Any understanding words he could have uttered would have only brought on the deluge; obviously he knew her well enough to realize she would hate to cry in public.

By the time Matt and Charlotte left the lobby downstairs and walked across the parking lot to his car, she had managed to compose herself. Even so, while they dined in a quiet little restaurant, he had to remind her frequently that she had to eat something. She knew that. Tomorrow promised to be a long day, and if only for her aunt's sake, she realized she needed to keep up her own strength. Still, it wasn't easy to swallow, considering the hard lump of unshed tears that seemed lodged in her throat.

After dinner, while driving to his house, Matt said very little unless Charlotte herself initiated a conversation. His brand of silent comfort was what she needed, especially since he continued to let her hold on tightly to his hand. When they got home, however, and went into the study, Charlotte couldn't be still long enough to hold on to anything. It was only nine o'clock, much too early to go to bed with any hope of going to sleep, and fear and worry made her flit around the room like a restless spirit.

"Can you get in touch with your parents?" Matt finally asked. "They'd want to know about the surgery, I'm sure."

"I know," she said, "but they were in one of the Chinese provinces, and it may take a while for my original telegram to reach them. I'm sure they'll call when they can." Tired of pacing, Charlotte sank down on the sofa. She picked up the large hoop that held the embroidery she had been doing and tried to focus her attention on that. After pricking her finger three times with the needle, she laid the hoop aside with a sigh.

"Have a drink with me," Matt suggested, going to the mahogany whiskey cabinet. "Just something light. Might help you relax."

With a grateful smile she declined. For some time after that she sat still, staring unseeingly into the flames in the fireplace. Countless memories of Louisa crowded her mind, memories of how much fun her great-aunt and uncle both had been during her childhood, and memories just as pleasant of more recent times. A very precious aspect of her life would be irretrievably lost if Aunt Lou . . . No! She wouldn't even think of that possibility. It was pessimistic and selfish to think about what she might lose. But she was so scared.

She jumped up and began drifting around the room again. She passed the chair where Matt had sat down again, and stopped when he reached out one hand. Her fingers grazed across his palm, then were caught firmly in his, and it seemed as if some of his strength transferred to her.

"It's nearly eleven," he told her as she stood. "I think you should go to bed now. Maybe you'll go right

158

to sleep." He walked her upstairs, left her at the doorway, and went on to the next one, which was his.

Over an hour later Charlotte was still awake. Fear was building inside her, and she switched on the bedside lamp, threw back the covers, and got up to wander the bedroom awhile.

Less than five minutes later her door was opened and Matt stepped inside, carrying a cut-glass tumbler. "I heard you moving around," he said softly, coming to her. "I think you'd better have this drink now. It'll relax you, though I went very light on the whiskey."

Their fingers touched when she took the glass from him. "Thank you for bringing it," she said after a tentative sip. "You're really being so kind."

"I've tried to tell you I'm not an ogre," he replied half seriously, seating himself on the edge of the bed. "Now, try to drink all of that." And he stayed to see that she did. When she took the final sip and the remnants of the ice clinked against the bottom of the glass, he got up and took it out of her hand. "Get back in bed now. You'll be able to sleep."

Watching him walk toward her door, Charlotte stood too. "Matt," she called, her hands moving toward him when he turned around. "I . . . don't think I can stand to be alone all night. Would . . . could you stay with me?"

His answering smile was indulgent and tender. "Of course, Charlotte. All you had to do was ask."

After putting the glass on top of her vanity, he shed his robe and tossed it across the foot of her bed. When she was lying down, he turned out the lamp and got under the covers with her.

Charlotte immediately felt more secure and less

afraid. His warmth enveloped her, and she snuggled close to him when he turned her onto her side, facing him. One muscular arm rested around her narrow waist, and soon after he began to stroke her back, she fell asleep.

Before seven the next morning Charlotte visited her aunt. Drowsy from the sedation she had already been given, Louisa smiled sleepily. "Well, this is the big day isn't it? I want you to know I'm not afraid. And I don't want you to be either. But promise me something. If . . . I don't make it, transplant one of those pretty little cedar saplings from beside the lodge to your mama's front yard. Then whenever you see it, you think of me."

Charlotte sobbed. Before she could prevent them, tears overflowed her eyes and streamed down her cheeks.

"I'm sorry, dear; I didn't mean to upset you," Louisa said, patting Charlotte's hand where it was clenched around the bed railing. "It was just an idea that popped into my mind. I didn't think it would make you cry."

"You just stop talking to me about transplanting trees; there won't be any need to do that," Charlotte murmured, leaning down to kiss Louisa's cheek. "This surgery's going to make you fit as a fiddle again."

Louisa smiled at hearing one of her own favorite sayings. "Fit as a fiddle. All right, dear, if you say so, I believe it."

Having succeeded in staunching the flow of tears, Charlotte smiled. "I'd better go now. You rest, and I'll see you in a little while."

"A little while," Louisa repeated drowsily.

Charlotte tiptoed out of the cubicle and past the nurse's station. When she found Matt waiting for her in the corridor, her tears began to flow again.

He frowned and pulled her to him. "What is it, love?"

Haltingly, she told him what Louisa had said about transplanting a tree, and when he murmured understandingly, her tears commenced again. He drew her into a secluded alcove beside the bank of elevators. Her head resting against his chest, she tried to stop sobbing as he gently stroked her hair.

"Let yourself cry," he whispered comfortingly. "That's what you need to do."

"I just didn't expect her to say something like that. But I shouldn't have let myself get so upset," Charlotte mumbled. "It's so silly of me. I'm sorry. I usually don't cry like this."

"Stop trying to be so tough. I've seen you cry before."

"But I started crying in front of Aunt Lou. I shouldn't have done that. I probably upset her terribly."

"Or maybe she understands better how much she means to you. That might make her fight for life," Matt suggested. "And the will to survive is vital."

Heartened by his words, Charlotte stood still while he used the corner of his handkerchief to wipe the tears from her cheeks. "I'm okay now," she said, though the smile she gave him was wan. "I know you have to get to your office, so go ahead. I'll be fine."

"It's not an absolute necessity for me to go in today." He started walking her toward the solarium. "I'll stay here."

161

The hours creeped by. Charlotte had known the surgery would take some time, but she began to feel she had been waiting in the solarium an eternity. Insisting they have lunch downstairs, Matt told one of the cardiac nurses where they would be, but when they returned, she had no message for them. It was nearly three o'clock when Dr. Nathan finally appeared, still in surgical greens, his expression unreadable. Moving slowly from the window toward him, Charlotte wished desperately his face showed some indication of how the surgery had gone. Finally he inclined his head in a brief nod and smiled, though cautiously. Charlotte felt faint with the relief that flooded through her, and she was grateful for Matt's supportive arm around her waist as the doctor stopped in front of them.

"She survived the surgery in fairly good condition," he began. "There were some touch and go moments when her vital signs had us a bit worried."

"But the surgery was a success?" Charlotte questioned. "And she'll be all right now?"

Dr. Nathan didn't want to be that committal. "She should be, if no complications develop within the next forty-eight hours or so."

"When may Charlotte see her?" Matt interceded. "I'm sure that's the question she intended to ask next."

His wry observation seemed to break a certain tension, and Dr. Nathan smiled, and even went so far as to pat Charlotte's shoulder. "She's in recovery now, but when she's brought back to her room, you may see her for a minute or two. She'll still be groggy from the anesthesia, so don't expect much response."

"You've already given me more than I expected," Charlotte confessed with a tremulous smile. "Doctor, how can I ever thank you?"

"I'll send you a bill," he quipped, and left them smiling at the well-worn joke.

Since the worst was over, Charlotte insisted Matt go to his office for a while, and when he returned for her about six o'clock, they went together to see her aunt for a moment. Louisa was unaware of their presence, though she mumbled in sleep. But her color was good, and Charlotte felt reassured.

Dinner that evening was far different than it had been the night before. Charlotte was relaxed and more her usual self than she had been in days. When she and Matt returned to his house, she couldn't contain her relief, and as he settled himself in the leather chair in the study, she left the sofa and leaned down over the back of his chair, her hands touching his shoulders. "I know Aunt Lou isn't completely out of the woods yet, but I really believe everything's going to be all right."

Taking hold of her wrist, Matt brought her around the chair and down onto his lap. "I think Lou will be all right too," he agreed softly, his magnetic eyes holding hers. "But there's still the airport. And I wonder if you or she can avoid being bitter about it."

Charlotte's smile faded. "I don't know. I guess I haven't thought about the airport much since Aunt Lou's been so ill. Her life was all that mattered, and I guess it's too soon to start worrying about the airport again."

"That will work out too. You'll see," Matt whispered, lifting her hair away from her neck to kiss her. When she trembled, he took her fully into his arms

163

and sought her mouth, his lips moving with evocative lightness against the soft full shape of hers. His hand swept over her, exploring, and familiar passion glinted in his eyes when he drew away slightly and looked down at her. "Tonight you stay with me in my bed," he said, rising easily from the chair with her in his arms. "I need you now, Charlotte."

And she needed him too, though her need was much more than physical. His kindness the last few days had served to strengthen her love for him, until now she doubted she could deny him anything. All she wanted was to be close to him, to give her love, and to pretend for just a little while that he could love her in return.

CHAPTER NINE

Five days after surgery Louisa was transferred from cardiac care to a regular ward. Charlotte no longer had to remain at the center all day just to visit her aunt for a few minutes every hour or so. Consequently, on Friday, the first day of Louisa's liberation from her cubicle in cardiac care, Charlotte spent the entire morning by her aunt's side, then left immediately following lunch, promising to be back again after dinner. While driving out to Matt's, however, she suddenly changed her plans. She and Matt had dined in restaurants almost every night, but tonight, she decided, she would prepare a meal at his house. She could go back to visit Louisa before dinner rather than after, so they could relax by the fireplace all evening.

Pleased with her idea, Charlotte stopped by a supermarket and purchased a sirloin tip roast and fresh vegetables to go with it. At a florist's she bought a bouquet of flowers to grace the table. Later, at Matt's, she had a long hot bath and luxuriated in the first relaxing afternoon she had spent in quite some time. At four thirty she put the roast into the oven and started out of the house, but stopped suddenly. She had almost forgotten to leave Matt a note, telling him where she was and when she'd be back and asking him to check the roast. Hurrying into his study, she sought a piece of paper on his desk and sat down in his chair with the memo pad she found. She started to flip back the first sheet, which had a note scribbled on it, when the words "Royal County property" suddenly seemed to leap up at her. She swiftly scanned the note: "Four o'clock Friday; sign transfer of deed to Royal County property."

Charlotte swallowed convulsively and for a moment could hardly breathe. The memo pad slipped from her fingers and dropped onto the desktop again, and she put her face in her hands. Everytime she began trusting Matt, something like this happened to make her realize what a fool she was being. The meaning of the note was all too clear. Though he had sworn he never planned to develop the land surrounding the meadow and his house, he was selling the property now—for a tremendous sum of money no doubt.

"You never learn, do you?" she asked herself aloud. Her breath was expelled in a startled gasp as a deep voice suddenly broke the silence.

"Never learn what?" Matt questioned, striding into the study as she jerked up her head. "Didn't mean to frighten you. I thought you must have heard me come in."

"I didn't. I was preoccupied." With a flick of her finger Charlotte sent the memo pad sliding across the smooth surface of the desk, and it teetered on the edge for a second before falling to the floor at Matt's feet. While he bent to retrieve it, she stood, and when he straightened and looked at the note, then at her, her eyes were dark with reproach. "I don't know why I'm

166

surprised, but I am. I suspected you wanted to make a huge profit on that land, but you vowed you had no intention of developing it. I was beginning to really believe that, but now—"

Matt shook his head. "But I'm not developing the property, Charlotte."

"What you're doing is no different. You're selling it to someone who will develop it," she retorted, anguish in her voice and her face. "How can you do it? That beautiful house, that lovely unspoiled land. How can you let all that go? Is making a profit so important to you?"

"You're getting upset about nothing," Matt said, coming around the desk, frowning as she backed away from him. "Charlotte, this is ridiculous. Just listen—"

Raking a hand through her hair, she shook her head. "I think I've listened to you too many times already. And dunce that I am, I usually fall for the line you hand me. So please spare me any more honeyed words. I've made enough of a fool of myself for one day, deciding you'd like dinner at home and rushing around trying to get it started before going to see Aunt Lou early. I was just on my way out, but I wanted to leave you a note. That's how I came across your little reminder to transfer the deed. Ironic, isn't it?"

Stalking her as she moved away, he finally trapped her in a corner of the room, and by placing a hand on the walls on either side of her, effectively barred her escape. "If you're finished hurling accusations, there's something I have to say," he began, his voice edged with impatience. "Something you should know about that deed transfer I signed today."

She tried to duck under one arm, and he simply moved it down to keep her imprisoned. "I don't want to hear it," she asserted icily, glaring up at him. At the moment anger at herself and him overrode even the pain she felt. "Would you be so kind as to let me go? I really don't want to listen to anything you have to say. I'd probably believe you, and I'm tired of amusing you with my gullibility."

"I'm not amused, Charlotte. But no matter how long I have to keep you in this corner, you're going to hear what I have to say."

She threw her hands up against his chest and tried to push him away. "Let me go! I won't listen to you. I know all I need to already. You may do a good job of pretending differently at times, but you're still one of those men who cares only about profits and your career. You're just like Brad."

The contours of Matt's face tightened, and his eyes narrowed to fiery amber slits. Powerful fingers encircled her delicate wrists; he pinned her hands against his chest, and with a step forward, pressed her back against the wall behind her. "I'm damn tired of being compared to that nitwit. I never want to hear his name mentioned again. But I can see you're in no mood to be reasonable right now. So go on to see Lou, and when we have dinner here as you planned, we can talk this over."

Charlotte's anger faded away, leaving her cold, empty, desolate. "There's nothing to talk about now," she reiterated dully. "I know too much and I have to get away from you. Since my parents are coming to Denver tomorrow, Aunt Lou won't need me, so I'm going home to Colorado Springs."

"If that's what you want, fine. Do what you damn well please," Matt said harshly, releasing her and moving aside. With unbridled mockery, he extended a hand in a flourish. "Go then. I'm not going to stop you."

"I never expected you to," she whispered, her lips twisting self-derisively. "I must be crazy. I know what you are and what you're capable of doing. But . . . God help me, I still love you. It's insanity."

Matt's relentless expression didn't alter. Standing very still, hands thrust deep into the pockets of his trousers, he simply stared down at her. "It's getting late," he said at last, his words clipped. "If you plan to see Lou before dinner, you'd better go now."

She nodded. Eyes lowered and stinging with the threat of tears, she stepped past him and went to retrieve her purse from his desk. At the study doorway she paused a second. "There's a roast in the oven. You'd better check it from time to time."

With that she left the house. It was only after she got into her car that she let a soft sob escape her lips as she rested her forehead against the cold steering wheel.

On the way to the medical center Charlotte forced herself to concentrate on driving cautiously, and retreated into the blessed numbness creeping over her. But it didn't do much to dull the stabbing pain that ripped through her chest when she thought of leaving Matt tomorrow, a pain she knew she would have to endure because she had to leave.

By the time Charlotte stepped off the hospital elevator and walked down the corridor to her aunt's room, she had managed to arrange her face into fairly composed lines. Sheer determination helped her smile brightly at Louisa, who was sitting up in bed, looking quite chipper.

"Aunt Lou, you look so good," she commented honestly and with relief as she leaned over to kiss her cheek. "Your color's even better tonight than it was when I left this afternoon. I bet some handsome doctor's been in here flirting with you."

"Don't talk nonsense. No doctor's been flirting with me," Louisa chided good-naturedly. "I'm happy because I'm glad to see you. Always am, especially if the visit's unexpected. Aren't you a bit early tonight?"

Nodding, Charlotte sat down on the chair by the bed, unaware of how tense she looked perched on the edge. "I decided to come now, then make dinner for Matt at his house." She made a great show of examining her fingernails. "I thought he might like that."

"Well, I'm sure he will. I think it's a fine idea," Louisa said, eyeing her niece speculatively. "Now, suppose you tell me what's bothering you."

Charlotte's eyes widened. "Bothering me? Why, nothing."

Clicking her tongue against the back of her front teeth, Louisa shook her head. "You can't fool me, honey. Ever since you were a little thing I could tell when something was troubling you, no matter how hard you tried to hide it. You get this kinda lost look in your eyes and it's there right now. So what's the matter? You and Matt had a lovers' quarrel?"

"You do see right through me, don't you?" Charlotte murmured, her answering smile bleak. "I tried so hard to hide my feelings. How could you tell I was falling in love with him?"

"It was my heart that was weak, not my eyes," Louisa said pertly, but her expression sobered abruptly. "Besides, it was pretty clear you loved him when you started sleeping with him in his room."

Charlotte met her aunt's wise old eyes directly, then shook her head and smiled ruefully. "You really don't miss a thing that's going on, do you? I can't say I'm ashamed of what happened . . . even now, I'm not. But if I offended you by staying in Matt's room, then I'm sorry."

"Honey, the world was different when I was your age, but that doesn't mean I live in the past. These days things have changed, and I know young people even live together before they get married. But I guess as long as they love each other—"

"You have that half right. I love Matt," Charlotte cut in softly, hurt darkening her eyes to a deep green. "But he doesn't love me. I'm not sure he can love anybody. I guess what astounds me more than anything else is how I allowed myself to get so involved with a man lacking in compassion."

"Lacking in— Charlotte Jordan, what's ailing you?" Louisa exclaimed softly, a sharp frown creasing her brow. "I've never heard such foolishness. Matt's probably the warmest, most caring young man I've ever met."

"Oh, Aunt Lou, you just don't know everything. I have to admit Matt can put on a good act, but he's just pretending he's kind and caring."

"Pretending? Oh, what nonsense. How could he be pretending when he—"

"I guess I'd better just tell you the truth before you hear it from someone else." Charlotte twisted her

171

hands together in her lap. "You know, of course, that Matt's meadow property was one of the possible sites for the airport. But he said it wasn't as suitable as the plateau. Well, I was afraid he might just be saying that because he wanted to develop his land—it's ideal for a ski resort—but he swore he had no plans for developing it. That wasn't really true. He's not going to develop it himself. But I found out that this very afternoon he was transferring the deed to someone else. He's sold that beautiful house and the land to a developer! And I know he must have been paid a tremendous price, so I'll always have to wonder if he sacrificed your lodge and you just so he could make a huge profit."

Louisa was staring at her niece, her mouth open in total disbelief. At last she snapped her teeth together and shook her head. "Well, laws, Charlotte, this beats anything I've ever heard. I thought you knew."

"Knew what?"

"I reckon if you'd told Matt about this crazy notion of yours, he would have told you."

"Matt knows I know exactly what he's done. I told him so right before I came here. So what could he have told me? I already know the whole sordid truth."

"You accused him of all these things and he still didn't tell you?" Louisa asked bewilderedly. "Well, that doesn't make much sense."

"What doesn't? Tell me what?" Charlotte repeated, remaining calm and patient in deference to her aunt's weakened condition. "I'm afraid you've lost me."

"You sure do have everything turned around. I don't know why that boy didn't tell you, but since he didn't, I will." With a knowing smile Louisa clasped

172

her hands just below her bosom, in preparation for her announcement. "Judging by the wild ideas you've been having, what I'm going to say will sure surprise you."

"I have no idea what you're talking about," Charlotte said, striving not to sound as exasperated as she felt. "But I certainly wish you'd tell me."

"Okay. Matt didn't sell his property. He deeded it over to me. Well, what he did was trade his place for the lodge and my land, but only for my lifetime. When I'm gone, his place will belong to him again and the lodge will go to my heir—you. That's what he's done, plain and simple."

Charlotte had never heard anything less plain and simple in her life. At first she was too stunned to speak, though her mind was racing. What was Matt up to now? Could this be some devious plot to cheat Aunt Lou out of her property? No, of course not. Despite all her doubts about Matt, Charlotte didn't believe he would swindle an elderly woman. Yet what did this property trade mean? She didn't understand at all, and lifted a hand in a helpless, uncertain gesture, afraid to ask the question poised on the tip of her tongue, but knowing she had to.

"You signed the lodge over to Matt?" she asked her aunt, her voice choked. "Did . . . did you read the papers you signed?"

Louisa gave a somewhat impatient snort. "Well, I wasn't born yesterday, dear. I always read anything I sign. Besides, I had a lawyer. The other day, when Matt first talked to me about this, he insisted I get a lawyer to represent my interests."

"You mean you've known Matt planned to do this

173

for days?" Charlotte exclaimed, more perplexed than ever. "Why didn't you mention anything about it to me?"

"He didn't want me to. Wanted to surprise you. He thought you'd be here this afternoon when he had his lawyer and mine stop by so we could settle everything. But you left right after lunch, and I couldn't stop you without letting you know something was going on. I just figured Matt would tell you this evening, but I guess after that fuss the two of you had, he decided not to."

Total confusion written on her face, Charlotte got up, walked to the window, then paced back. "I still don't understand any of this. Why did Matt trade his property for yours? How can that arrangement possibly benefit him?"

Louisa lifted her eyes heavenward. "You really ought to stop thinking the worst of him, dear," she scolded gently. "I'm trying to tell you what a nice thing he's done. He said he knew moving into his house wouldn't make up to me for losing the lodge, but that at least I'd have peace and quiet and a secluded place for my guests to come. Well, I didn't want to accept his offer at first; I guess I'm too proud and it seemed like charity. But he said he'd feel awful if I didn't agree, and I got to thinking about how noisy that airport will be. I'll miss the lodge, but at his place I won't have planes zooming over my head. Besides, we agreed I could visit the lodge whenever I want, as long as his room at his place is always available to him. So you see, honey, he *is* warm and caring. And you must be blind not to see that."

As the truth finally sank in, Charlotte groaned

aloud and nearly collapsed onto the chair. "Oh, my God," she cried, and ducked her head in shame for all the accusations she had hurled at Matt. No wonder he had reacted furiously, and practically said he couldn't care less if she left his house. How he must despise her now. And she couldn't blame him if he did. After all, he'd done something exceptionally kind for her aunt, and was called a profiteer for his trouble. Wringing her hands, Charlotte looked back up at Louisa. "Oh, I didn't know. I have been blind, Aunt Lou. I've never really trusted Matt because of what happened with Brad, I guess. And Matt seemed so cold and business-like when I first met him. Oh, that's not a good excuse, I know, but . . . oh, hell, I just never expected him to do something like this for anyone, even you, fond of you as he's always seemed."

"I can't believe you're being such a little ninny," Louisa declared with complete candor. She wagged a finger at her niece. "How can you think Matt did this for me? Oh, he probably is fond of me, but I'm still just an old lady he's only known a little while. And he's only a man, not a saint. He didn't go to all the trouble of trading his place for mine just to make *me* feel better. Silly child, he did it for you. He knew how upset you were about what the airport was going to mean to me. And you sit there and say he's not in love with you." She sniffed. "If he doesn't love you, then why does he care so much about trying to make you happy?"

"And if he does love me, why didn't he tell me the truth this afternoon?" Charlotte shot back, bur-geoning hope and an oppressive fear beginning to play tug-of-war with her emotions. She pressed her fingers against her temples to ease the ache the battle was creating there. "He could have made me listen if he'd really wanted to. But he didn't even mention transferring the deed to you."

"Too proud to probably," Louisa speculated, her expression gentling as she reached for her niece's hand and patted it. "Sounds to me like you said some pretty terrible things to him. Maybe he got tired of trying to defend himself."

"I've ruined everything, haven't I?" Charlotte muttered.

"That's nonsense. You can't give up so easily."

"But you didn't see his face this afternoon, Aunt Lou! I've never seen him so angry. I told him I had to get away from him and that I was leaving for Colorado Springs tomorrow, and he told me to do as I damn well please, that he wouldn't try to stop me. So it's over, and it's all my fault."

"That was just his pride talking," Louisa argued. "When you tell him you're sorry—"

"I don't think I can face him now. He was so disgusted with me this afternoon that I doubt he'll accept my apology. And if he didn't, I don't think I could stand it."

"You're going to have to try, child. Since you're in the wrong, you'll have to risk your pride."

Charlotte shook her head. "I just can't."

"You can. Now go and do it," Louisa said flatly, releasing her hand. "Don't worry about leaving me early. I'm tired anyway and ready for a little nap. So run along now, dear." Watching as Charlotte obediently stood, she smiled lovingly. "You've never been a coward, honey, and you can't afford to start being one now. If you don't do everything you can to make this up to Matt, you'll regret it to your dying day. You know that, don't you?"

"But what happens to me if an apology to Matt doesn't do any good?" Charlotte asked bleakly, really expecting no answer as she kissed her aunt good-bye.

CHAPTER TEN

Half an hour later Charlotte pulled into Matt's driveway, her stomach aflutter with mounting dread. After stopping in front of his house, she sat clutching the steering wheel for several long moments. Although Louisa was obviously confident that an apology would mend the rift in Charlotte's relationship with Matt, Charlotte herself was plagued with doubts. She had experienced his anger this afternoon, and recalling how indifferent he had seemed even when she had confessed she loved him, she was engulfed in despair. What was the point in subjecting herself to more heartache, when he apparently didn't care very much what she felt for him? The point was that she owed him an apology and had to try to make amends for not trusting him, she told herself sternly, gathering up the tattered remnants of her courage and stiffening her spine. Opening the door before she could change her mind again, she got out of the car and walked up the flagstone path to the portico.

At the door Charlotte hesitated, however, reluctant to just walk into Matt's house. Instead she lifted the brass ring of the knocker and tapped it lightly, unconsciously holding her breath as she waited for what seemed an eternity. At last the door opened and Matt stood on the threshold, his lean face devoid of expression. He moved aside, and as she entered and stepped past him, he said, "It wasn't locked, Charlotte."

"I know but . . . well, I didn't think I should just walk in uninvited after . . . after the way we . . . argued this afternoon," she admitted, bringing up the subject in the hope that he would want to discuss their disagreement.

Matt simply shrugged. He politely helped her out of her coat, hung it away in the hall closet, then walked back toward the kitchen without a word. With a droop to her shoulders, Charlotte followed. When she entered the kitchen, she found Matt slicing fresh mushrooms into a salad he had prepared, and when she also discovered he had put potatoes into the oven to bake, she tried to give him a teasing smile.

"How industrious you are. But then, you've always known your way around a kitchen, haven't you?"

He glanced up briefly from the salad to look at her, then turned his attention to his task again. "I'm a competent enough cook, I guess. At any rate, I've never poisoned myself."

His words and his attitude were so icy that Charlotte suddenly shivered. Peering into the oven at the roast, grateful for the warmth that rushed out at her, she added somewhat weakly, "Well, I appreciate your help, although I had . . . sort of planned on playing chef tonight so you could relax."

"Suit yourself, then. It's all yours," was his unconcerned response. Dropping the knife and half a mushroom into the wooden salad bowl, he wiped his hands on a towel then strode out of the kitchen.

Twenty minutes later Charlotte served the meal in the dining room, hovering near the table as Matt silently poured rosé wine. Still with no more than impersonal politeness, he held her chair, and after she sat down, seated himself across from her. They dined by candlelight, but even the soft warm glow did nothing to take the chill out of the atmosphere. Matt spoke only once, inquiring how Louisa was feeling, and when Charlotte gave him an answer, the silence commenced again.

Her nerves becoming increasingly frazzled, Charlotte succumbed to the tension that seemed almost tangible between them. Her throat went tight; it was nearly impossible to swallow the little bit of food she forced herself to chew, and even the tiny sips of wine she took made her feel as if she were choking. Displeasure with her seemed to emanate from Matt, and she wasn't sure how much longer she could endure such obvious contempt. Whatever slim hopes she had entered the house with earlier had dwindled. Matt was acting as if she bored him to distraction, and it was apparent that he didn't care enough about her to give her another chance. Not that she really deserved one, she thought. She had been such a fool, she could see that now. But it was too late, and pain at the realization ripped through her chest. Her eyes filled with tears, and she lowered her head so Matt couldn't see them.

The excruciating meal ended at last. Taking her at her word, Matt retired to his study, allowing her to clean up alone. She dawdled over the chore, reluctant to join him. Somehow, despite his indifference, she still had to offer her apology, although she knew mere words would never compensate for the lack of faith she had shown in him. Finally she forced herself to walk into the study, only to find Matt immersed in a book. When he took no notice of her, she sank down on the edge of the sofa, manufacturing a soft nervous cough to gain his attention. Yet when he looked up, lifting his brows questioningly, all the words tumbling around in her mind could find no voice. She could only stare at him, the emotional stranglehold on her throat tightening unmercifully until she could hardly breathe. Since she didn't speak, he did.

"Delicious dinner, Charlotte," he commented perfunctorily, closing his book on one long finger to keep his place. Settling down more comfortably in his chair, he stretched his legs out before him, acting as if he were perfectly relaxed. "Oh, by the way, what time do you plan to leave for Colorado Springs tomorrow?"

Charlotte winced. "I—I hadn't actually thought about what time I'd leave," she answered, relieved her voice sounded almost normal, at least to her own ears. "Why do you ask? Is it important for you to know a precise time?"

"No. Just wondered," he said with a careless shrug, then opened his book again.

Suddenly Charlotte could withstand his torturous contempt no longer. She moved swiftly to the end of the sofa near his chair and leaned toward him. One hand fluttered out to touch his arm, but as she felt his muscles tense beneath her fingertips, she allowed the hand to drop away. "Oh, Matt, I'm sorry. So very sorry," she whispered earnestly, her eyes dark with contrition. "Please try to forgive me for not trusting you. I know I should have, but I guess I was just

181

afraid to, and I jumped to too many stupid conclusions. I don't blame you for being angry and upset with me, considering all the stupid things I said. I can't begin to tell you how I regret all of them."

She had expected some response from him, but none was forthcoming. Instead he simply looked steadily at her, and his silence intensified her guilt.

"Why didn't you tell me this afternoon what you'd done for Aunt Lou?" Charlotte exclaimed urgently. "Why did you let me accuse you of only caring about profits when you could have stopped me by telling me the truth?"

Matt's gaze skimmed over her, but he remained silent until she thought she would explode.

"I think I'd better leave for Colorado Springs right now," she muttered almost incoherently, starting to rise. "I can see you don't want me here any longer, so I'll go tonight. Good-bye, Matt."

She was halfway up when Matt sprang forward in his chair, grabbed her by her arms, and pulled her to her knees on the carpet in front of him. Rough hands slipped up and over her shoulders, easily overcoming her frantic effort to rise and escape him. A strange light glinted in his amber eyes.

"Not so fast, Charlotte," he murmured, his voice low and rough. "I'm not going to let you run away as easily as that. You owe me more than apologies for all your doubts about me. Now it's time for you to pay up." Ignoring her startled protest, he pulled her up into his arms, crushing her hard against him.

His fingers slipped through her hair and his thumbs lifted her chin. She was completely in his power, held fast, and she was so astounded by the savage intensity her apology had unleashed, that she was suddenly and completely still. Her eyes searched his face, widening with disbelief when she found only an unswerving intent to conquer in his features, but even her sharp intake of breath did nothing to deter Matt. Danger glittered like gold in his eyes and a purposeful smile moved the mouth that came down to cover her own. He kissed her again and again and each time his mouth was more masterfully demanding, slightly twisting the softness of her lips, devouring their sweetness.

Charlotte trembled violently in his embrace and moaned softly as her body traitorously responded to the unbridled passion anger had aroused in him. His kisses were like a succession of electric shocks, and exquisite sensations scattered over every inch of her skin. His hands swept over her playing across her breasts until they surged tautly against his palms, then traveled down to span her waist. When his lean, strong fingers spread caressingly across her flat abdomen, crumpling the soft wool of her skirt and drawing it far up her legs, Charlotte could only cling weakly to him, unable to resist when his hand dropped down to one upper thigh.

His mouth took hers then, the tip of his tongue tasting the sensitive inner flesh of her lower lip until her breathing became increasingly ragged. He lifted his head slightly. She opened her eyes and his face filled her vision as she whispered huskily, "Is this your revenge?"

"Mmm, and how delightful revenge can be," he whispered back before his lips covered hers again. His caresses became more intimate, asserting his right of possession, and his desire seemed to flare out of control as he pulled her blouse open. He pushed the fabric off her shoulders and brushed her straps aside, his lips following the fiery trail his fingers had blazed. A low groan came from deep in his throat as he unhooked the front closure of her lacy bra and peeled the cups away, baring her breasts to the touch of his hands and mouth.

As he scattered nipping kisses around one rose-tinted peak and then the other, thrill after thrill ran rampantly up and down her spine. Her own free hand stroked feverishly over the taut muscles of his back while a central warmth intensified within her and surged like fire through her veins. Matt jerked down the zipper of her skirt, arched her hips upward slightly, and pulled the garment off completely. Charlotte's breath caught in a gasp. He had never been less gentle with her, yet she still loved him and needed to give herself to him. How could she respond to him when all he wanted now was revenge? she wondered bleakly, unable to suppress the tears that sprang without warning to her eyes and soon overflowed onto her cheeks. Then a soft sob escaped her.

"Crying, Charlotte?" Matt uttered roughly, releasing her lips from another of his kisses to gaze down at her. "Why?"

"I don't want it to be this way," she muttered, her tears still flowing. "I . . . don't want to let you use me."

"I've never used you. I'm not using you now," he whispered. "You want me as much as I want you."

Charlotte shook her head. "But you only want to take out your anger on me."

"Maybe it began as anger, but now it's . . ." Shaking his head, he kissed away the tears on her cheeks, then brushed his lips across hers, leaving in their wake a faint salty taste. "It's time you learned, love, that a man can't always be exceptionally gentle. Right now I want you so badly I—".

"You *want* me. That's all, and it isn't enough. I need . . . more."

"Tell me why you need more," he coaxed softly. "Tell me now."

"Because I love you. So very much," she breathed, and became mesmerized by the triumphant smile that touched the corners of his mouth.

"I had to hear you say it again," he said, rubbing the balls of his thumbs over her cheekbones. "I'll always want to hear you say it, because despite what you think, I love you too. Do you trust me enough to believe that?"

With a nod and a muffled cry of happiness, Charlotte wrapped her arms tightly around his neck and pressed close against him. "You should have told me what you were doing for Aunt Lou this afternoon," she scolded halfheartedly as her lips sought the strongly beating pulse in his neck. "Why didn't you just tell me the truth?"

Winding a thick swathe of her hair around one hand, he tilted her face up and gazed into her eyes. "The fact is I was fed up with trying to convince you to have some faith in me. Besides," he added succinctly, "I seriously doubted you'd believe me if I told you I'd traded my property for Lou's."

Charlotte winced. "Maybe I wouldn't have. Probably not. But everything's different now, and I really am sorry I couldn't trust you before. Try to understand, though, that learning you owned the meadow confused me terribly. It did seem like a conflict of interest since you were the one choosing the airport site. And I guess I just couldn't give you the benefit of the doubt, mainly because of Brad."

"You're not supposed to mention his name to me, remember?" Matt said, laying a fingertip against her lips. "That young idiot caused you to give me one hell of a time since the first day we met, so let's just forget about him."

"He's forgotten now that I know you're not at all like him," she promised, unbuttoning first his vest, then his shirt, to run a hand lightly over his warm chest. "And as for the hell I gave you, maybe there's something I could do to make up for that."

"Oh, I have something specific in mind," he replied, smiling wickedly, his gaze roaming over the enticing contours of her bare upper body. "But first I want you to know that I want to marry you, as soon as possible. Now you have no reason to start doubting my intentions. That proposal proves they're honorable."

"No more doubts ever. I've learned my lesson," she said, lovingly tracing her fingertips along his mouth. And when he brought her arms up around his neck again, she moved close to him eagerly. "And I accept your proposal. There's nothing I want more than to be your wife."

For the next few minutes that followed, the silence in the room was broken only by a steady ticking of an antique grandfather clock in the corner and the muted endearments Matt uttered against Charlotte's lips as they clung together. At last, when his lingering kisses and possessive caresses had aroused her senses to a fever pitch, she nuzzled her cheek into the hollow of his shoulder to whisper breathlessly, "Matt, please. Take me to bed."

"Too far away," he whispered back, his voice revealingly uneven as he lifted her up in his arms to lay her gently down on the rug before the fireplace. He came down onto his side next to her, a wealth of tenderness and love warming his eyes. "I want you now. I can't wait any longer."

Charlotte watched through the thick fringe of her lowered lashes as he swiftly finished undressing her, then stripped his own clothes off. For a long moment he knelt beside her, gazing at her smooth satiny skin until she caught his hand and brought it up to rest in the warm hollow between her breasts.

"God, I love you," he groaned, moving swiftly above her, one knee easing hers apart. "So much, Charlotte."

The plush carpet was a sensuous texture to her moving legs, and the softness beneath her and the hardness of his body above her transported her to that plane of being she could only share with him. His fingers slipped into the glorious thickness of her hair, his palm cupping one side of her face, and when his hand beneath her hips arched her upward to receive him, her mouth sought his. Her sigh of ecstasy feathered over his lips and her fingernails scraped lightly down his broad back as he took her gently but insistently.

Desire and mutual love entwined to become inseparable, and for Charlotte, every pleasure was heightened by his whispered assurances. Able to give herself without inhibition or fear of future heartache, she delighted in her newly discovered ability to arouse him, and they were swept up together in a spiral of intensifying pleasure. The ultimate peak of ecstasy they shared in their love brought them both deeper fulfillment than they'd ever known before.

Considerably later, upstairs in Matt's bed, Charlotte nestled close to him, one hand lazily curved around the side of his neck. She smiled as he grazed a kiss over her tousled hair.

"As far as I know, we only have to have blood tests before we can get married. I don't think there's a waiting period in this state," said Matt, moving his arm more securely around her shoulders. "So since you'll be Mrs. Royall by the day after tomorrow at the latest, we'd better start thinking about where we want to spend our honeymoon."

"I know where I'd like to go. The meadow house. Aunt Lou won't be moving in until she's stronger. And since that's where you first seduced me," she added, smiling as he chuckled, "I can't think of a more romantic place. Can you?"

"Sounds like the perfect way to begin our marriage," he agreed. "But you do realize that if we go there, we could possibly be snowed in for the whole winter?"

"Of course I realize that. Why else do you think I suggested it?"

Six months later Charlotte and Matt walked hand in hand behind Louisa as she led them through the garden behind the stone house.

"Have you ever seen so many different kinds of flowers?" Louisa asked, bubbling with enthusiasm. "I tell you it's a treat for me to come out here every morning and find something new in bloom. So many perennials. And have you ever seen anything as pretty as all these roses? My, someone must have really loved this garden."

"My grandmother had a green thumb," Matt explained, draping an arm across his wife's shoulders to draw her closer to his side. "She used to spend almost all her time out here. We'd tease her by saying we wouldn't know her without a trowel in her hand."

"I'm beginning to know how she felt. I come out here so much these days that I'm afraid I'm going to start neglecting my guests," Louisa admitted with a sheepish smile, then tapped a hand against her cheek. "And speaking of guests, the three arriving here tomorrow won't get anything to eat if I don't get busy. You two stay and enjoy the fresh air while I go in and call in an order for some groceries."

As Louisa walked back toward the house, Matt and Charlotte sat down on a wrought-iron bench, facing the rolling hills that tumbled down to the edge of the greening meadow.

"Well, what do you think? Is Lou really happy here?" Matt asked, stretching his legs out as Charlotte rested her head against his shoulder. "She seems to get along fine with the housekeeper we hired to help her. All in all, she acts content."

"I really think she is. Oh, she misses the lodge, I'm sure of that, but much less now that construction's started on the airport. She knows nothing will ever be quite the same around the plateau again and she's grateful for the peace and quiet here." Leaning her head back, Charlotte smiled up at Matt. "And in case you hadn't noticed, she adores you for letting her have this place. And so do I, though there are many other reasons why I love you like crazy."

"Well, tonight when we go to bed, I'll make you give me the entire list," he promised. "And I have a list of my own about why I love you like crazy too. If you'd care to hear it . . ."

"No woman in her right mind would refuse an offer like that," Charlotte assured him, settling more comfortably in the circle of his arm. "I have to tell you though that Aunt Lou is a little disappointed in us about something else. It seems she's ready to become a great-great-aunt. When you were carrying our luggage up to our room, she asked me point-blank why I'm not pregnant."

Matt laughed. "And did you tell her it's because I have no intention of sharing you with anyone just yet?"

"No. Actually I told her it's because *I* don't want to share *you.*"

"Same thing," Matt replied, leaning down to brush a loving kiss across her parted lips. "We agree that babies will come later. Isn't it amazing how alike we are in our thoughts, especially considering the fact that you once believed we had almost nothing in common?"

Charlotte grimaced. "You're never going to let me forget that I completely misjudged you, are you?"

"No chance. You're far too much fun to tease," he admitted, then his expression grew serious. "You know, now that I look back, I can see my life was rather lonely before I met you."

"So was mine. But now that we're together, I know exactly where I belong."

"Yes, with me," Matt said with an endearing smile. "And don't forget that or you'll soon discover what a possessive man I can be."

"I wouldn't want it any other way," Charlotte whispered, smiling back as Matt gathered her into his arms.